THE

IVY ASHER

Copyright © 2020 Ivy Asher

All rights reserved. This book or parts thereof may not be reproduced in any form, stored in any retrieval system, or transmitted in any form by any means—electronic, mechanical, photocopy, recording, or otherwise—without prior written permission of the author, except in cases of a reviewer quoting brief passages in a review.

This is a work of fiction. Names, characters, places, and incidents either are the products of the author's imagination or are used fictitiously. Any resemblance to actual persons, living or dead, businesses, companies, events, or locales is entirely coincidental.

Edited by Polished Perfection

Cover Design by Nichole Witholder at Rainy Day Artwork

For Sunny...you know why, winky face and chumus.

PROLOGUE

Warning growls and screeches reach out from behind us, making it clear that Pigeon and I are being hunted. We zip through the sky, but I can feel on the wind that one of our pursuers is gaining on the left. We veer to the right to avoid contact for as long as possible. The evasive maneuver seems to work, and Pigeon and I maintain our lead and continue to search for something that helps us get these fuckers off our tail. We round a mountain, and the bright flash of sun on water beams up at us. It's momentarily blinding and keeps us from seeing the webbed mass that comes shooting up into the sky until it's almost on us.

Pigeon shrieks and barely avoids the net, and I realize too late that we weren't outmaneuvering the gryphons chasing us, we were letting ourselves be herded by them. *Fuck!* Another net comes screaming up into the sky, and by some miracle, Pigeon does this crazy tuck roll thing that keeps us out of its clutches. But as we recover from the epic dodge we just executed, a third net comes speeding for us, and this one hits its mark.

The net slams into us and wraps around us like a snake

does its prey. Pigeon can't extend her wings to catch the current, and we start to fall out of the sky, careening toward the water. We're spinning as we fall, and the torque of it leaves me completely disoriented. One second I'm staring at the sky, the next I can spot the water we're about to crash into any minute now. We're rolling with such force that it steals all ability to make any sounds, and we can't even scream as the water's surface looms even closer, bringing with it promises of pain.

Pigeon and I crash into the water, and it hurts almost as much as when Zeph the sky shadow smashed us into the ground. The heavy net surrounding us immediately pulls us further down, and I feel the terror and panic that surge through Pigeon as we're dragged against our will toward the bottom. I yank on the tether that connects us, demanding Pigeon's attention, and try to pull her back into me. The squares of the net that's doing its best to drown us look big enough for me to try and fit through, but I have to get Pigeon to relinquish control so we can shift and I can try to get out.

I slam against her a couple times, and it finally gets her attention. She quickly hands me the reins, and we shift back into me. I work to untangle the dense net from around me, and I lose the bag that was strapped to my chest. The map flashes in my mind as the bag sinks out of reach, but losing the map will be the least of our problems if I can't get us out of the net. I'm just small enough to wiggle my way out through the mesh of the dense rope. I kick frantically for the surface of the water, my lungs burning and my head starting to swim with black spots.

I barely break out of the water before I gasp, breathing in air and water at the same time. I cough violently trying to purge my lungs of the lake I just aspirated. Strong arms pluck me from the rippling depths, but there's nothing I can do to free myself from my captor as I work to clear my lungs of water and fill them with air instead. I'm flown to the bank of the lake, and I continue to cough and try to take in my surroundings. I can tell by how Pigeon has receded inside of me that she's hurt, and I know that saving our ass is just up to me now.

I'm set gently on the sand of the shore, and I immediately reach back with my left hand and grab the junk of whoever is holding me. As expected, he drops his hold and reaches down to protect himself. This gives me the perfect opportunity to whirl around and punch him in the throat with my other hand. I'm up and sprinting away as he collapses in on himself, and I send up a silent thank you to Sutton and his training.

A massive gryphon slams down into the sand in front of me, and I shriek in surprise. I try to change directions, but another gryphon cuts me off. I stop and spin, looking for a way out, but I'm cut off by gryphons at every angle. A couple of them shift out of their gryphon form, and I take that moment to charge the smallest gryphon of the group. He snaps at me, which is exactly what I hoped for. I dodge his hooked beak, just barely, and land a punch to the side of his head.

I scream through clenched teeth as fire shoots up my hand into my arm. I feel like I just punched a fucking boulder. I lose the momentum of the attack as pain vibrates up my arm, and before the gryphon I assaulted can move to tear me apart, someone is pulling me away from him.

My arm is throbbing, but I unleash all of the fight left in me as I try to get out of the grasp of whoever is holding on to me.

"Caught a live one, didn't we now," an amused voice announces. Chuckles sound off around me, and I struggle even harder to break free.

"Go tell the commander we caught something interesting," the same guy orders, and the gryphon to my right pumps its wings and flies away.

"Highborn from the looks of it. Is she marked?" another voice asks, and I'm immediately shoved forward.

I'm bent over at the waist, completely naked thanks to the sudden shift into Pigeon earlier. Whoever is holding me is also naked, and I feel his limp dick skim my ass and start to grow firmer. I release a warning growl that goes ignored as someone brushes hair from the back of my neck and checks the skin there.

"No mark," the first voice declares, and I'm pulled back up. I'm brought face to face with another naked massive shifter who has long straight black hair, blue eyes, and a dimple in his clean shaven chin. He brushes the white strands of my damp hair out of my face, and his eyes light up with interest as he takes me in.

I snarl at him, but this only seems to amuse him. The guy holding me tries to stop my continued struggling to get out of his hold, and I wince when he yanks on my hurt hand. *Note to self, if we survive this, never punch a shifted gryphon in the face again.* The blue-eyed guy in front of me doesn't miss my pained response, and he reaches out and grabs my chin in an effort to make me go still.

"You'll just hurt yourself worse if you keep that up, flower," he chides, his eyes locked on mine.

I'm still not sure if staring contests with gryphons hold the same weight as they do with wolves, but I fix my lavender gaze on him and refuse to look away. I stop struggling, the fight slowly leaving my body, and the absence of it invites shock and exhaustion to flood me.

"That's a girl," he tells me, the firm grip he has on my chin softening ever so slightly, but he doesn't let go. "Now what's a pretty purple flower like yourself doing way out here?"

His bright blue eyes run over my features like he's searching for answers, and I internally cheer as he's the first to break eye contact with me.

"You don't look like a rebel," he observes, picking up a strand of my hair. "And yet you bear no mark."

I debate the best way to handle this situation. My initial instinct is to stay quiet, but as I subtly pull in a deep inhale of the blue-eyed shifter in front of me, it confirms my suspicions. He has the windy lilac scent of a gryphon, but that same hint of citrus that the hunters that captured me and Zeph in the woods had. I thought maybe it was because those gryphons were related somehow, but now I'm realizing that the citrus smell might be what the vow does to a gryphon's scent.

These shifters are the Avowed, and maybe, just maybe, the truth of how I got here will work on them like it did with the Hidden. I stare into the curious blue eyes of the shifter in front of me and hope they don't have an Ami that will see the parts of my story that I'm hiding. I'll just have to deal with that later if it happens.

"My name is Falon Solei Umbra," I offer. I take a second to look around at the strange gryphons surrounding me and let fear and confusion leak into my eyes. "I woke up in this strange place a couple of days ago, and I've been trying to figure out how to get back home ever since."

"And where's home, flower?" Blue Eyes asks me, concern leaking out of his tone, but it does little to mask the cunning glint in his eyes.

"Colorado."

A large tan gryphon slams down onto the sand on my right, and the force with which he lands sends vibrations through the ground up into my legs. His arrival pulls my thoughts away from the plausible cover story I'm trying to pull from my ass. This must be the commander that Blue Eyes requested. That thought turns to ash in my mouth as another massive, well-muscled shifter touches down gracefully on the bank just behind Blue Eyes. Large gray and white wings give a quick flap and are then quickly folded back, giving me a clear line of sight at a familiar face. My eyes go wide with shock and then quickly narrow with stupefied confusion.

What the fuck is Ryn doing here, and why does he smell different?

1

"Well, well, well, what do we have here, *soldier*?" Ryn asks, and the other gryphon shifter with the blue eyes and chin dimple chuckles.

My gaze snaps from Ryn for a second to take in the amusement that lights up the blue-eyed shifter's eyes, but I don't watch him long enough to gauge what that amusement means. I focus on Ryn as he steps closer to me, confusion warring with a warm feeling that moves through me. I expect Pigeon to wake up and flood me with some unwelcome feeling of desire or happiness, but she's quiet. That alone has worry coursing through me as I search Ryn's gray stare for some sign of recognition… There is none.

I'm tempted to ask *what the fuck is going on*, but thankfully, I still have some sense intact. If this is Ryn—and not some evil twin he forgot to mention—my announcing that I know him isn't going to go over well for either one of us. Instead, I activate damsel mode. I shy away from Ryn's large form like I'm terrified of him. It's not a hard stretch from how I'm actually feeling. I have no fucking clue what is going on or just what I've landed myself in the middle of.

I bump back against the large shifter who is still holding

onto me from behind. All *that* does is remind me of the erection he has pressed into my back. I immediately arch as far away as I can from the unwelcome boner and lean toward the large black-haired, blue-eyed shifter in front of me. I don't miss a flash of what I think is satisfaction in his bright blue gaze before he clears it and turns to answer Ryn's question.

"I'm not quite sure yet, Commander," he responds with a curious almost sarcastic inflection on the word *commander*. "This female ran from a patrol that spotted her flying east of here. She was netted and then fished from the water. She's unmarked and has a lovely tale about how she's not from here and is just trying to get home," Blue Eyes finishes, a sly smile stretching across his full lips.

"Is that right? And where exactly is *home*?" Ryn asks, leveling me with his stormy gray gaze.

I watch as anger strikes through his eyes, quick as lightning, before giving way to a cool indifference. *Shit.* Maybe this is an evil twin, or maybe that look is because I'm here and not back in the Eyrie like he expects me to be. My nostrils flare as I try to scent him again now that he's closer. It smells like Ryn, but not...and I have no fucking clue what that means.

"Some place called Colerdo," Blue Eyes supplies when I don't make any effort to answer mystery Ryn's question.

The maroon Narwagh armor that mystery Ryn is wearing squeaks as he motions for the gryphon who's holding me to move. My erection clad captor releases me and moves away. Ryn steps around me, and an odd sensation tingles through my body when his fingertip skims over my shoulder and slowly moves the hair away from the back of my neck. He's armed to the teeth, which should probably set off some kind of alarm. Instead, I have to tamp down on the shiver that courses through my body, and I'm trying—

and failing—to keep my nipples from morphing into diamonds, and goose bumps from rising in the wake of his touch.

"So we're to believe that the Amaranthine Mountain spirits are gifting us with beautiful, highborn, unmarked females now?" Ryn asks, his featherlight caress moving from my neck and trailing suggestively down my spine.

Snickers sound off around me, and I work not to show how uncomfortable I am right now.

"All hail the Thais Fairies if that's the case," Blue Eyes announces, and more laughter bubbles up from the gryphon soldiers surrounding me.

"No wonder the rebel scum have been spotted more and more in this area. Who can blame them with such gifts wandering about?" someone out of sight comments, and Ryn is so close to me now that I can feel the laughter vibrating from his chest into my back.

Unease unfurls within me, and the jeering laughter all around me makes me want to run.

Mystery Ryn bends so that his lips are inches away from the shell of my ear. "Too bad, little sparrow, that I was always taught never to trust anything that seemed too good to be true," he announces, and panic roars through me.

I'm not sure exactly what sets it off—maybe it's the use of Zeph's nickname for me or the thinly veiled threat he just mock whispered in my ear—but everything slows. Before I even know what I'm doing, I reach back and pull a dagger that's strapped to Ryn's side from its sheath. I surge forward and press the newly acquired blade to the throat of the massive blue-eyed and dimple-chinned gryphon shifter in front of me. The amusement quickly fades from his sparkly blue gaze, and I watch the shock seep in as I press my dagger into his corded neck.

Everyone around me freezes.

I look around, terrified as other shifters press closer, and I scream at them not to take another step closer.

"I don't know who you are," I shout out the half lie, my voice manic and brimming with genuine fear. "I just want to go home," I beg, my hand shaking as I hold the dagger to Blue Eyes' throat. He'll probably snap me in half when this is done, but I have to risk it. My options are nonexistent. There's nowhere to run; I'm surrounded.

"I'm going to find my way home, and if any of you try to stop me, this dimple-chinned motherfucker is going to die," I threaten.

Blue Eyes' gives an amused snort, and my eyes snap to his. "What the fuck do you find so funny?" I snarl, irritation swooping in to embrace my distress.

"I can see that you're scared, flower, but you and I both know you're not going to slit my throat," he states evenly, the corners of his ample lips turning up into a confident smile.

The smirk's presence pisses me off.

"If it will get me home and away from wherever the fuck I am, I will," I challenge, pressing the blade harder against the warm skin of his throat.

His annoying smile widens, but something flashes in his eyes. His gaze morphs, and I can see and feel the gryphon in him staring back at me. The blue of his eyes flickers, like the connection is bad and they can't settle on a color. I'm so hypnotized by it—and the heat that's suddenly surging through me— that I don't even fight when a huge tan muscled arm circles my neck from behind. I'm forcefully jerked back from the dimple-chinned asshole. The choke hold around my throat tightens as a fire blazes through my blood. I'm lifted off the ground, and the pressure on my throat increases to dangerous levels. I panic and scramble to find any kind of footing as I'm choked.

Surprise penetrates my hysteria when I bring my hands

up to claw at the arm around my neck and I realize that I still have the dagger in my grip. I drop my arm, twist the blade, and then slam it as hard as I can into the torso of whoever is trying to kill me. A pain-filled roar rents the air all around me, and I shove the blade into someone up to the hilt. The pressure on my windpipe decreases slightly. I release my hold on the dagger and proceed to claw with both hands at the meaty arm around my neck and gasp for air.

"Pigeon!" I scream for all I'm worth. *"Pigeon, please, I need you!"*

Nothing.

Frustration and worry burn through me, but I don't have time to focus on that. I need to get away! I snarl and scramble and do everything I can to free myself, but it's no use. The shock of my stabbing has worn off, and the arm around my neck tightens. I can't get enough oxygen into my lungs again, and terror is overriding every sensible thought in my head.

I don't want to die!

"Looks like our little flower here is just full of surprises," Blue Eyes says, and Ryn grunts behind me. "Ease up, Commander, I think you're hurting her," Blue Eyes warns when I stop making a gurgling whimper and go silent.

"I'm just putting her to sleep. It'll be easier to get her, and us, back to Kestrel in one piece if she's out," Ryn offers, and I put everything I've got into one last effort to break his hold.

I can't be taken to Kestrel City. I need to get out of here and back home! I reach up with one hand to try and gouge out an eyeball, but I can't find his eyes. I reach back with my other arm and search for the dagger I stabbed him with. I almost get my fingers around it when a large hand grabs mine. Blue eyes fill my darkening vision, and I can feel tears dripping down my cheeks.

"It's okay, flower. Just rest. No one is going to hurt you," he reassures me, his eyes soft and his tone gentle.

I glare at him and mentally cuss him out. *No one is going to hurt me? Fuck him.* Tell that to the arm around my neck that's slowly choking me out. My body gives one last jerking protest, and then everything starts to go black.

Motherfucker.

* * *

"Awlon, is this really the only way?" my mother asks, her voice and eyes filled with devastation.

I'm groggy as I try to look around. What is happening? I'm so tired. The room is cloaked in night, and I can't figure out why my parents are waking me up.

"I wish it weren't the way either, Noor, but it has to be done. They give her away, and we can't afford that." Dad runs his hands through his black hair. His face is strained, and he looks completely stricken. "I can't understand how she has them. They don't normally show up this early. I thought we'd have until puberty, but we don't," he declares, his tone haunted.

"Can't we just keep them covered?" mom asks.

"Long sleeves aren't going to hide them forever, Noor. Her eyes and hair are already an issue, and we haven't been able to track down another cladding stone. What would you have me do, Noor? Tell me another way, and I'll do it."

My dad's voice is desperate as he pleads with my mother, and I can just make out through the haze that's coating my brain that my mom and dad are hugging. I try to move, but I'm stiff and clammy. All I can remember is hurting and then waking up to my parents fighting. I whimper, and my mother shushes me and rests her palm on my forehead.

"It's okay, Falon, we're here. It'll all be over soon," she reassures me, pressing a kiss to the crown of my head. "Just do it, Awlon, before she comes to even more. I just hope she forgives us one day."

My mom is crying, but I can't grasp anything that's happening around me. It's like I'm surrounded by wispy thoughts and people, and I can't hold on to anyone or anything long enough to help me understand.

"Mommy," I mumble, scared, and she pulls me into her lap and begins to rock me.

She starts to sing my favorite bedtime song, and her clear soothing voice instantly calms me. I relax into her arms, the beat of her heart against my ear and her song lulling me back to sleep. And then there's pain. So much pain. Pain and screaming and then...blackness.

I shake my head to clear it of the overwhelming phantom pain. My heart hammers in my chest as I struggle to pull oxygen into my lungs. I try to focus on the dream-memories, to try and understand what they mean, but the details start to slip through my fingers like warm desert sand.

What the fuck was that?

I press back against cool smooth stone. I lift my head and survey my surroundings. I'm shrouded in shadows in the corner of what used to be my room in the cliff castle.

How the hell did I get here?

My lavender gaze runs over the lines of Zeph's massive muscled body. He's sitting on the corner of the large bed, bent over something in his hands.

Shit. Did Ryn bring me here? Is Zeph going to make good on his promise to kill me if he ever sees me again?

I hold my breath, not sure what to do or say. Zeph silently strokes the fabric he holds in his hands with his thumbs, and I realize after staring at him for a moment that he's holding the dress I wore the night we hooked up. It's torn and tattered—which is to be expected after what happened that night—but I'm taken aback by the fabric's presence and the reverent touch that Zeph is administering to it. I haven't given any thought to where that dress went, and I can't understand why Zeph would have it.

It's almost like he's mourning, and that makes no fucking sense to me.

I jump, startled, when Zeph releases an angry roar. The peace in the room is shattered by the terrible sound, and Zeph shreds the soft fabric in his hands and throws it across the room. He rises off the bed and then turns and upends it. The frame and mattress crash against the pillars that separate the room from the balcony, and the wood of the bed splinters and goes flying.

He roars again, like the sound alone will purge whatever it is that's haunting him, and rips the headboard apart like it's made of popsicle sticks. I watch the tantrum from the corner, baffled by what could have set it off. I'm simultaneously judging this display of pain and anger while feeling drawn to comfort him and make it stop. He shreds the soft yellow case on the pillow and then throws it. The pillow hits the wall a foot from my head, and I jump again.

The movement has Zeph's eyes snapping to mine in the corner. He breathes hard from the epic shit fit he's in the middle of throwing, and his honey-hued gaze takes me in warily. I don't move or speak. We both just stand there like statues.

"Are you here?" he asks me, disbelief bleeding through his tone.

He takes a step toward me and then pauses as if he's suddenly unsure. I open my mouth to say something when I feel a sharp tug in my abdomen. I gasp at the unusual sensation and look down, expecting a hook or something to be sticking out of me. There's nothing there. I place my hands on my stomach as another strange tug pulls at my insides. It's not painful so much as uncomfortable, but I have no idea what the hell is going on.

I look up, my worried wide eyes landing back on Zeph's uncertain golden stare. And then just like that, I'm yanked out of the room, like a fish on a hook, by some unseen force.

I wake up, the sound of Zeph screaming my name still ringing in my ears. I slowly blink away the grogginess and roll from my side to my back. The clanking of chains echoes off the dark stone walls, and I look down to see that my feet are shackled. I release a groan and try to take in my dimly lit surroundings.

Shit.

I'm pretty sure I'm in some kind of dungeon.

"About time you stopped frolicking in your dreams and came back to the real world."

I yelp at the unexpected voice in the cell with me and turn to find Ryn leaning casually in a dark corner. It takes me a moment to wake all the way up and absorb where I most likely am, and then another beat to recall why. I fix Ryn with a look that promises pain and then leap for him.

"You fucking prick! I'm going to kill you!"

2

I surge up from the ground like some demonic frog, hell-bent on strangling Ryn with the smug look on his face and my bare hands. I don't get very far. The chains I momentarily forgot were around my ankles put a quick stop to my vengeance-filled trajectory. I'm snapped back like a dog on a leash by the unwelcome tether, and I face plant on the cold stone of the cell's floor, with a very pitiful sounding *oomph*.

"Rutting Cynas, Falon, what do you think you're doing?" Ryn asks me as he scoops me up in his arms and sets me back down on a stone ledge that I'm pretty sure is supposed to serve as a bed.

"Trying to kill you; what does it look like I'm doing?" I ask incredulously, as I push out of his hold and rub at the bruises I know are forming on my shoulders from the graceful swan dive into stone I just executed.

Fucking chains.

"Where exactly am I?" I demand as I bat Ryn's hand away when he reaches for me. I give him a clear warning-filled look and scoot as far away from him as possible.

He looks hurt by that, but fuck him.

"You're in Kestrel City. You'll be brought in front of the Syta as soon as your guard returns from taking a shit and realizes that you're awake."

"Syta as in Zeph?" I ask him as I rub at my ankles and the tender skin being rubbed away by the chains attached there. I realize that, at some point between being choked out by Ryn and arriving at this place, someone put a long shirt on me. It smells like Ryn, and I'm tempted to rip it off and throw it at him.

"No, you'll be meeting, Lazza, the Syta of the Avowed," Ryn explains, his gray eyes looking over me in search of something.

"What the fuck are you doing here, Ryn?" I demand, standing up and trying to tamp down the shiver working its way up my spine from the cold of the stone bench.

"I could ask you the same thing, Falon. Last I checked, you vowed to stay in the Eyrie until I returned," Ryn snaps back, the concern dimming in his eyes as it's replaced with anger.

"Fuck off, Ryn, you shot me out of the sky and then put me in a fucking choke hold until I blacked out. If anyone has a right to be pissed here, it's not you," I growl at him.

Ryn shushes me and then looks over his shoulder. We both go quiet as he listens for something before turning back to me.

"Do you think I enjoyed finding you naked in the middle of an Avowed hunting party? Falon, you attacked the worst possible target you could have attacked. I had to think fast. You're lucky to even be alive," he snarls back at me.

"Ryn! What the fuck are you doing here? Aren't these people the enemy? Does Zeph know?" I whisper-screech at him.

He rushes forward and presses me back against the wall,

his hand over my mouth. His massive body pins me in place and fury boils through me.

"Falon, I know you're mad, but you have to be quiet. I can't get caught down here, and no one can know that we know each other. Your life—and mine—depends on it. Do you understand?" he angry-whispers in my ear.

He pulls back and studies me, waiting for me to concede or acknowledge his warning.

I just stare at him, my gaze furious. Ryn huffs out a resigned breath and leans his forehead against mine. I really fucking hate that his mere presence still soothes me after everything that's happened. What's worse is that Pigeon is still down for the count, so I can't even blame the warm and fuzzies on her.

"Zeph knows I'm here, Falon. I would never betray him. I've been spying for the Hidden for a long time," Ryn confides.

I let his words sink in. I wish somehow this information made me feel better, but it doesn't. He removes his hand from my mouth, the action a clear indication that he thinks it's my turn to start explaining, and looks at me expectantly.

I debate what to tell him. He just said he would never betray Zeph. Does that mean if Zeph wants me dead, then Ryn is automatically on board with that too? I play back in my mind what happened and try to pick out the safe things to clue Ryn in on. Zeph reacted badly to my whole Oath Breaker news, so I decide to pluck that detail out along with several others.

"It's a long story," I start, "but the short of it is that Zeph told me to leave...and never come back."

Ryn's eyes widen with surprise, and his gray gaze bounces back and forth between my resigned lavender stare. He can see the truth there, and he shakes his head in disbelief.

"I'm going to kill him," Ryn declares, and he steps away from me and runs his fingers through his light brown hair in frustration. "Why the rut would he do that?" he asks me, suddenly pacing around the cell like some caged beast.

A distant clanging interrupts my response, and he freezes. We both listen, although I have no idea what I'm listening for. Ryn steps back into my personal bubble and cups both of my cheeks.

"I have to go, Falon. When the guard comes back, he'll check on you, and then you'll be called up to answer to the Syta. You can't tell them anything about me or the time you spent with the Hidden. If you do, we'll both be tortured and killed."

His warning and his gaze burn white hot through me.

"I wasn't planning on doing that even before you landed on the beach and fucked me up," I growl quietly. "I'll stick with the *I don't know how I got here* story," I pause and realize there's just one big problem with that plan. "Ryn, do they have anyone like Ami here? Anyone who can see that I'm full of shit?" I ask, a new wave of worry coursing through me.

"They do, but the seer that will be in there today will cover for you," he answers simply, like it's just that easy.

A soft bird-like whistle floats in from the hallway, and Ryn's head snaps in the direction of the metal door.

"I have to go, but don't worry. You've intrigued the Altern of the Avowed, and you'll be fine. Just stick to the story, and I'll get you out of here soon, okay?"

Ryn doesn't wait for me to respond. His lips crash down on mine, sealing his promise, and I can't help the moan that his mouth coaxes from mine.

Why do all the assholes here have to be such good fucking kissers?

He pulls away and slips soundlessly out of the door. I internally facepalm.

That was unlocked this whole time? What the fuck?

I reach for the handle and give it a yank. Screw waiting for Ryn to get me out of here, maybe I can be my own knight in Narwagh armor. Of course the fucking door doesn't budge now. I release it, defeated, and then huff out a long irritated sigh.

Footsteps sound off in the distance, and I sit back down on the stone bed shelf and wait. I reach inside of myself to try and check on Pigeon, but there's no indication that there's anyone else inside this body other than me. I search harder for her presence. *Could the fall have hurt her permanently?* Is that even possible? I know that Pigeon and I are separate in ways that the other gryphons aren't, but I have no idea what exactly that means for us. Can she die while I still remain? Can the opposite happen?

I just barely touch on what feels like a deeply wounded consciousness when the clanging of metal pulls me from my thoughts and internal efforts. I look up to see a small metal panel pull back on the door. Dark eyes peer in at me, and I can see surprise register in them for a split second before the panel is quickly closed and heavy footfall leads away from my cell.

I swing my feet, not liking the heavy feel of the metal that's linked around my ankles, and study the walls of my cage. I don't know what I expect to find—claw marks, rats, some kind of tally situation—but the walls are dark and bare, and the cell clean and cold. I'm not sure how long I wait, but the sound of marching fills my ears, and my adrenaline kicks in and hikes my anxiety up to a whole new unhelpful level.

The rhythmic sound of heavy footsteps is ominous. I swear it sounds more like the boom of war drums signaling my impending death. I try to control my breathing and to keep from panicking, but I'm not doing so well. I curl up in the corner of the stone bed shelf and try to make myself as little as possible. I hate that I feel this way again, helpless, out of control, scared, but no matter what I do, I just keep finding myself here.

Sutton's voice fills my mind, and I try to focus on the things he taught me. I tell myself to focus on what I *can* control, to be smart about this. I give myself a little pep talk to try and stem the anxiety, but it's only half working. The door to my cell flies open, and I jump and whimper at the sudden booming sound.

I really need to stop being so fucking jumpy all of the time, it's not helping my rep.

Large armored guards file into the small space, and suddenly I don't want to feel as small as possible; I want to be as big as Zeph and rip them all apart.

"You have been called to appear before the Syta. Rise, and you will be escorted there in peace. Refuse, and...well, you will be taken there anyway," a guard informs me.

I snort, unable to help it. The dude really needs to work on the climax of his delivery. I unfold myself on the bench bed and stand up. The guard gives me an approving nod and kneels to remove the shackles from my feet. He tuts when he sees the abrasions on my ankles. I don't say anything. I'm pretty sure I did that to myself when I went for Ryn, but if he wants to feel bad for me, I'm perfectly fine with that. He can get in line right behind me, and we'll drink wine and throw an epic pity party.

"Follow me," he instructs, his tone softer, and then he moves out of the cell.

I'm instantly surrounded by big beefy guards and escorted down a hallway. The dungeon looks like it's torch lit, but when I get close, I can see that what I thought was fire is just a strange moving light. Whatever it is, the flickering of the non-flames still causes the shadows to play tricks on my eyes.

It's surprisingly quiet down here. There's no tortured screams or begging from other prisoners for help. I don't even spot another person. It's like I have my own private wing of the dungeon. There's no moaning or groaning like I'd expect. There's just the sound of the guards' heavy boots on the stone floor as we wind our way through the eerie quiet.

Eventually a staircase appears, and I'm led up several flights. I'm starting to seriously rethink my need for cardio when we stop climbing and instead branch off down a wide hallway. We stop at a gargantuan heavy-looking door, and the lead guard proceeds to do some kind of secret knock. The metal squeals in protest as it opens, and I'm ripped from the dimly lit dungeon and forced into the light.

I shrink back, blinded by the overwhelming and painful brightness. I try to stop and shield my eyes, but the guards push me to keep moving. I blink rapidly in an effort to adjust, but my eyes well up from the illumination's assault.

"Keep walking," a guard demands, like his shoving me around isn't enough and he feels the need to add useless narration.

I'm body checked again from the side when I stumble, and I bite back the nasty words I want to let loose. I want to snap at them to hold their fucking horses for a second until I'm no longer blind, but aside from the guy who took off my chains, I don't get the impression that any of them have much of a compassionate side. I bite my tongue, but I can't quite swallow down the growl that bubbles up my throat. The lead guard looks back at me, seemingly amused by the sound, which of course just makes me growl even more.

"Keep purring, little kitten, it's music to our ears," he jeers.

I glare at him but tell myself not to engage. No good will come from pissing off someone who I might be dealing with for who knows how long. Yeah, I'm being taken to the Syta, but what happens after that? The cat-loving asshole could be my warden for all I know at this point—or my future torturer. I swallow down the bile that creeps up the back of my throat at that thought. What happens if I can't pull this off and they don't believe me?

What Zeph and Ryn put me through in order to interrogate me blazes forward in my mind. I shiver. I hope it doesn't get worse than that. I push those thoughts away and try to distract myself with my surroundings.

People move here and there, each of their strides filled with purpose as they make their way to some predetermined destination. No one pays me and my escorts much attention as I'm taken from a dungeon-bound hallway through a cavernous corridor. I'm surrounded by what looks like crystal and iron. The floor is the same cream stone that comprised the cliff castle, but the walls here are transparent. At first I think it's glass, but I quickly realize it must be something else. The clear surface is smooth like glass, but there's an unusual sparkle to it, and prisms dance in the corners of the massive translucent panes. Through the windowed walls, I can see crystalline high-rises all around us and a sliver of water between two large buildings.

It's like I'm staring at some kind of bejeweled city, and I'm not sure what to make of any of it. Unusual shaped towers of varying heights glisten and sparkle in the sun. It's so incredibly foreign and fantastical that I find myself feeling more lost than ever. Frustration surges through me that I was knocked out when I was brought here. How the fuck am I supposed to get my bearings or understand where

I am now in relation to where I was? My head swings around like a pendulum as I try to take everything in. I spot a few gryphons flying through open crystal-like windows, but not nearly as many of them soaring about as there were in the Eyrie.

My guard stops suddenly.

I'm so busy paying attention to my surroundings that I almost run into the back of the large shifter. A boom sounds on the other side of the closed entrance, and the tall iron doors in front of us slowly split. They groan ominously as they're opened, and fear and uncertainty surge through me. I take a deep breath and search for some of the brave I know I have tucked away somewhere inside me.

"Miss you, Pidge," I lament.

I can't help but send a silent plea to her for strength, even though I know it will go unanswered. I'm ushered inside of a room that makes me feel even more like I've landed in the middle of some kind of fairy tale city. The walls are the same iron bordered crystal, and they reach up several stories high into a dome above me. The room is easily the size of a football field and a half, and I'm tempted to scream out *echo* and listen to my voice bounce back to me over and over again. The clear walls to my side have some kind of magical fountain, and water pours tranquilly down them to collect in narrow lily pad covered pools below. Lotuses in every color imaginable bloom on the surface of the thin pools, and I catch sight of what I think is a fairy flitting from flower to flower.

I've never seen a fairy before, and I can't seem to tear my eyes from it. I can barely make out the flit of wings; beyond that, it looks like a ball of light bouncing around the plants and water like it's tending to them. I scan the rest of the magical waterfalls and pools, but I don't spot any other little balls of light.

There's no one else in here other than the group of guards around me and some other sentries standing here and there. I look around in awe, and I can't get over the magical feel saturating this place. It reminds me of an echo of something I felt in Vedan when I sat with Nadi in the overgrown gazebo. There, it was like I was feeling the loss of something, but here, I'm overwhelmed by how alive it all feels.

The iron and crystal surrounding me has an industrial look to it, and yet it merges seamlessly with the touches of nature and the magic sprinkled throughout the space. The details in this room look like they shouldn't fit together, but something about their essence feels the same, oddly enough.

I'm led deeper into the space until I'm standing almost at the far end of the long room, in front of several bulky, high-backed thrones. They appear to be made of the softest looking moss I've ever seen, and I have to fight the urge to step forward several feet and touch it. Really, I want to go full cat and rub all over it, but that's a level of weird I doubt these people are up for.

I look down and discover that the guards have stopped me just shy of a rug that's all grass. It looks like a living rug, and there are these delicate little purple flowers that trim the edges on every side.

Long black hair and blue eyes flash through my mind, and I try to blink away the image of the shifter that liked to call me flower. The feel of the knife in my hand when I held it to his throat comes to me unbidden. I'm sure wherever he is, he's not thinking of me as some sweet purple bloom anymore.

The guards all around me are silent as death, but out of nowhere, they straighten, standing a little taller and a hell of a lot stiffer. That slight movement is the only indication I get that something is happening. Quietly, people slowly pour into the room single file and take a seat in the soft mossy thrones. Women in barely-there dresses sit demurely, their eyes trained on the chair in the middle. Some old and wizened males enter, and I automatically peg them as the brains of this line up. They're followed by younger, muscled, and armor-clad males who I mark as the brawn.

My eyes narrow as I watch Ryn file in and claim a seat on the far left. How is he Hidden when he's clearly some kind of leader or royal here? He smirks at me, and before I can stop it, another growl starts up in my chest, and I take a step forward. The guards in front of me tense and move to block my advance.

Get a fucking grip, Falon. How about we don't invite a death sentence straight out of the gate.

Deep rumbling laughter fills the room, bouncing around the crystal surfaces and slowly getting absorbed by the greenery. A large chuckling shifter enters, his long straight white hair flowing behind him, and his smile accentuating the dimple in his chin. He looks familiar somehow, which doesn't make much sense. He has one blue eye and one purple eye, and they're filled with amusement as he takes me in.

Where the fuck do I know him from?

"What's so funny, little brother?" another male asks as he follows the laugher in.

This male has light gray hair with white streaks in it. It falls just to his shoulders, thick and arrow straight. His aqua-colored eyes watch the amused face of the male he called little brother. There's a cunning glint in his green-blue eyes, and it almost feels like he's hunting the male who I think looks familiar as he confidently strolls to the throne in the middle and sits down. So this must be the Syta.

The leader of the Avowed doesn't pay me any attention

as he settles in and adjusts his soft cream-colored tunic. Oddly, all eyes—except for apparently his little brother's—are fixed on him as if they're not allowed to look anywhere else until they've been given permission.

I don't know what to think of his arrival. I expected maybe an announcement or more fanfare involved in the entrance of the King of the Avowed. Instead, he just walks in casually as if whatever is about to happen is business as usual. What do I know, maybe it is. I realize I'm still growling quietly, and I immediately work to swallow it down.

Shit. Nice first impression, Falon. Just growl the whole time the leader enters.

I internally face palm and hope he doesn't take it personally.

"Sorry, brother, it couldn't be helped," the familiar male I still can't place starts. "I found our guest's response to the Commander amusing. It seems she doesn't take kindly to being rendered unconscious," he adds, his mismatched eyes sparkling as if he's letting me in on some inside joke.

Whatever it is, I don't get it, and I study him for a beat as I try to solve the puzzle. Is he secretly Hidden too? No, that can't be it. I would have remembered another Ouphe tainted gryphon aside from me and Ami. Especially another white-haired and purple-eyed highborn looking person like me in the Eyrie. Ami's face flares in my mind. I hope he's okay. I wonder what he and Tysa think about my leaving. Maybe I should have taken the time to say goodbye. Guilt stirs inside of me, but I push it away to deal with later. I focus on the row of moss covered thrones and try to figure out which one of them is the friendly lie detector-slash-seer that Ryn said would be present.

"Shall we get started?" the Syta asks, finally done primping and settling into his throne. His tone sounds bored, and I don't know if I should be offended or worried by that.

No one answers, which seems to be what he expects, and he gives a nod and finally turns his piercing gaze to me. I can't explain the feeling that washes through me when his eyes connect with mine. It's like I can feel his power, and it's hard as fuck not to buckle under the weight of it. There's a humming sensation that starts up just under my skin, and it's as if his power is calling to the power that exists in me.

It's not exactly a comfortable sensation. Our magics don't feel like old friends that hug and pat each other too hard on the back and start reminiscing about the good times. His magical touch has an arrogance and vitality to it. Mine feels more like an ancient grumpy presence that's pissed because someone just fucked with its nap. The Syta just stares at me, and I can't help but feel suddenly vulnerable, as if his stare alone has stripped me bare. I get the distinct impression that he's trying to hold on to something he's taken from me. Something that he has no right to. I don't exactly understand what all of this means, but the ancient power rolling inside of me feels like it wants to flex.

I drop my chin slightly and stare at the Syta, determined to give him a lesson in not touching things that don't belong to him. One of his eyebrows flicks up, intrigued, but the weird ass staring contest continues. The room is still, you could hear a pin drop, which is strange because I would think the waterfalls on the walls would make some kind of noise. I can see slight movement in my peripheral, but I don't dare pull my attention from the aqua stare fixed on me.

Challenge accepted. I just hope it doesn't get me killed.

3

"So it appears that what my brother and his soldiers have said is true," the Syta starts, like he's hoping his voice will snap me out of my fixed stare. "You are not marked, and I have no sway over you. They also tell me that you claim to not be from here, is that correct?" the Syta asks me, his eyes never blinking.

"Yes," I answer, simply tilting my head to the side slightly.

His casual mention of having no sway over me makes goose bumps rise on my arm, and I don't like the boulder of unease that now sits in the middle of my gut as I think about anyone else other than me having *sway* over what I do or say.

"So how do you explain your presence before us now then?" he queries, his tone skeptical.

"I can't explain how I'm here," I answer. "All I know is that one minute I was in a clearing in the world where I'm from, and the next minute I'm waking up in a land I've never seen before...with abilities that I never knew I had."

The male with the blue and purple eyes, sitting to the left of his brother the Syta, scoots forward in his seat. "What abilities?" he asks, naked interest in his tone and unusual eyes.

The Syta's stare narrows slightly, and then they flick briefly in the direction of his brother. I get the impression that he doesn't like that he was just interrupted, but I'm too focused on the fact that I just won an epic staring contest to pay much attention to the undertones of sibling rivalry. I turn my attention to the familiar little brother, and then a bitch-slap of recognition finally hits me.

He's the soldier I attacked. He's the one who called me flower.

"You look very different from the last time I saw you," I state, the comment half question and half exclamation.

"It wouldn't serve for the Avowed Altern to be roaming around enemy territory without a good disguise, now would it?" he tells me, a sly half-smile turning up the corner of his mouth.

"Enemy territory?" I ask, feigning confusion.

I'm tempted to blink a lot and play with the hem of the tunic shirt I'm draped in. Maybe it will up the *poor me* damsel thing I'm hoping they're buying, but I think the growling might have fucked up my chances of really pulling it off.

"Yes, Falon Solei Umbra, it seems you've landed yourself in what's about to be a war zone," the Syta announces, leaning back in his soft moss covered throne.

Do not look at Ryn. Do not look at Ryn.

"A war zone?" I repeat as if I'm some dumb broken parrot and haven't heard all of this before.

"Don't worry yourself about it, there's no doubt that we'll be victorious," the Syta declares arrogantly as he inspects his cuticles. "Back to the matter at hand, I believe my brother asked you a question."

Confusion takes over my face, and I rewind the conversation, trying to recall what I was asked.

"You mentioned that you had abilities here that you didn't know you had, I wanted to know what abilities?" the blue- and purple-eyed Altern of the Avowed reminds me.

"Oh right. Yeah, I thought I was a latent wolf shifter before I woke up here. It turns out that I'm neither latent or a wolf," I explain. I feel like a broken record going through all of this again and have to remind myself that they haven't heard it before, only the Hidden have.

I catch a subtle hand gesture from one of the scantily clad females to the right. Bingo. Looks like I know who the seer is now. I notice the gazes of several of the other seated shifters go from her back to me. I once again admonish myself not to look at Ryn just to see if everything is going according to plan.

"So you woke up here, and you've just been wandering around the Amaranthine Mountains ever since?" an elderly male asks me, his milky gaze soft.

"Yes, I've been trying to find my way home ever since."

I look as the female's hand goes from a fist to flat, and just like that, everyone in the room slightly relaxes. They believe me.

"Well, Falon, I don't know what act of fate brought you here, but now that you are, the Avowed claim you. You will now be one of us and enjoy all the protections and advantages that come with the Vow. I am Lazza, the Syta of the land and all of its inhabitants. My brother, Treno, who you've already met, serves as my Second and the rightful Altern. My Third and Fourth are Commander Ryn and Commander Voss."

Ryn nods at his introduction as does another female on the right, who I wouldn't have suspected as being a leader of any kind.

"The rest you'll meet as you adjust here. Saner will take you to get your mark. Once that's done, you'll be free to make a life for yourself here," Lazza tells me, like he's doing me some massive favor.

It's all so casual. Like he finds people all the time and just marks them and puts them to work. There's no discussion, no explanation, no concern over whether or not I want this or even understand what any of it means. It's like he expects me to fall at his feet and thank him for taking me in. Like I've been wandering through the mountains for days just hoping someone would claim me.

"But I don't want a life here; I want to go home," I interrupt, and the Syta's bemused gaze turns just a touch colder.

"And where is home? How do you propose to get there?" he asks flatly.

"I..." I trail off, biting back that I know enough to try and wing it. "I don't know," I finally say, and he smiles arrogantly at me.

"We can't have you wandering around. It's a surprise you even made it alive as far as you did. There are savages out there in the mountains. Be grateful that we were the ones who found you and not them," he snaps, and the room falls eerily silent once again. It's like the water doesn't even want to draw attention to itself, so it hits the mute button.

"Your place is now with us...as it should be," he adds, his aqua stare running over my tangled white hair and landing on my lavender eyes.

I see a glint of something in his gaze that I can't quite place, and unease pools in my belly.

"Saner, please escort our guest to receive her Vow and then to her new lodgings so she can clean up."

Fear breaks open inside of me, and I look around panicked. *The Vow.* That's what the Hidden have spent their existence avoiding. What did Tysa say about it? That it allows them to control you? *Fuck.* I can't let that happen. I need to get out of here. I back up and slam into a herculean sized guard behind me. I try to sidestep him, but huge hands come down on my shoulders to try to pin me in place.

Terrified, I look to Ryn. Is he really going to let them do this to me? His countenance is cold and disconnected, and I just barely stop myself from screaming out to him for help as another guard steps in to subdue me. This can't be happening. He can't just decide to mark me and that's that.

"Please don't," I shout as I'm hauled off my feet and caged in by muscled arms the size of my thighs. "Please, just let me go home! I have a life there. I don't want to be here!" I shriek as I'm carried out of the room.

Treno, the shifter I attacked, who apparently is the second in command here, shoots to his feet like my terror-filled screams just lassoed him and yanked him out of his throne against his will. He looks pained, but I don't know what to think of that before I'm taken away. The tall iron doors shut behind me, blocking him from view and sealing my fate.

Well, fuck that!

I fight...uselessly. I release a barrage of verbal abuses at the guard carrying me around like a sack of potatoes. I curse him, his friends, his family, and everyone's children's children's children. I get a couple good eye gouges in and am halfway to ripping off his nipple when he just passes me to an even bigger guard. I shamelessly resort to biting.

I don't pay any attention to where I'm being taken I'm so hell bent on trying to get out of the guard's hold. So when I'm dumped on my ass in what looks like some kind of church-like room, I'm surprised. A huge boot immediately pins me to the ground by my throat. I'm already struggling to catch my breath because this fucker just knocked the wind out of me when he threw me down; the boot to the throat is completely unnecessary.

Good thing I ripped out a chunk of the fucker's armpit hair just before he dropped me. I add that to the score board of hits and then squeal and try to get out from under his boot. I wrap my legs around his tree trunk thigh and go for a good junk hit, but he's too tall for me to connect properly. Fuck. Why didn't Sutton teach me how to get out of shit like this?

Fucking Gryphons and whatever growth hormone that makes them giants!

I gasp and sputter when the guard applies more pressure to my airway, but I can't stop fighting. I don't exactly know what the Vow is and what all it entails, but I don't want it. I have the sinking suspicion that it will mean that I can never get home, and I can't have that. It's the only thing I have to hang on to. That may be pathetic or delusional, but it is what it is.

Something hard and cold is pressed against my neck, and a slight stinging sensation there has me immediately going still. I pull my focus away from kicking in the guard's dick and realize that one of the women from the Syta's entourage is crouched next to me. And yep, she's holding some kind of knife to my throat.

"Leave us," she orders, her green eyes fixed on mine.

I realize quickly that it's the seer-slash-lie detector chick. Ryn said she'd turn a blind eye to my half-truths. Despite the knife at my neck, a flare of hope goes up inside of me. Ryn said he would get me out of here, and she must be it. I release a relieved breath, grateful that he wouldn't let this happen to me.

The guards that brought me here hesitate.

"I said leave," the woman barks out again, and this time, the mountain sized males hurry to listen.

Heavy footfall moves away from me. I lie still, the blade nestled against my throat as a door closes and the room grows quiet. I pant from my escape efforts and from fighting the guards, and wait for the green-eyed woman to tell me that it's time to run and get me out of here.

"Listen carefully, Ouphe Born," she starts, and a sinking feeling in my chest warns me that maybe she isn't the savior I was hoping for. "The Altern said we can't let them mark you, which means we have to do to you what we did for him. I'll mark you, but not with the Vow. It will be a dead marking. It will look and smell right, but nothing more. It will hurt, and we don't have time to waste."

At first I picture the mismatched eyes of the Avowed Altern and wonder why he'd be the one stepping in. But I quickly realize that she's talking about Ryn. She presses the knife harder against my neck, and I can feel warmth spill around the blade.

"Here's the thing, little one, you have to stay away from Lazza and his advisors at all costs. If they try the mark, they'll know it's not right, and you will have just exposed everyone who has one. Lazza doesn't know that we can do this, and if you're the one to reveal it to him, I'll kill you. Do you get me?" she asks, the question more of a growl as she pulls the dagger from my throat.

I give her a frenzied nod yes.

"Roll over," she commands, and she shoves my shoulders to hurry me into action before I can so much as blink and respond to the order.

I move the rest of the way to my stomach, and I feel the blade of the dagger she's holding slice through the top of the shirt I'm wearing. I want to protest because this is the only article of clothing I possess, and it'd be cool if she didn't shred it, but I worry she might get stabby, so I shut the fuck up. I feel her grip the back of my neck, and surprisingly there's heat where her palm and fingers meet my skin.

I gasp, and then I'm suddenly not there anymore.

It hurts so much. Why does it hurt? I struggle to get away from the hands holding me down in my bed. My screams are accompanied by a rhythmic chanting, but the burning I feel everywhere overshadows it all. I writhe and beg for it to stop. I can just make out my mom and dad.

"Mommy, please, it hurts!" I wail and struggle harder to get away from the hands and the pain they bring with them.

"Shhhh, I know, My Heart, it'll be over soon. Be strong, my girl. Be strong for mommy."

I keen and plead for it to stop, but it doesn't. The fire wants to eat me up whole, and no amount of screaming or begging will keep it from consuming me.

4

"Wake up," a growly female voice demands.

My cheek lights up with a stinging sensation, and I can feel someone shaking me.

"Wake up!" the voice orders again, and this time I get a hand up before she can slap me another time.

"What the hell?" I groggily ask as I come to.

I catch a flicker of relief in the female lie detector's green eyes before I look around and try to make sense of what's going on. I'm still in the weird chapel-esque room. There's an altar-like pulpit at the front of the room, and pews all lined up like they're ready and waiting to worship and watch whatever Vows or other bullshit goes down in here. This is the only room— aside from the dungeons—that I've seen that isn't capped by crystal walls and iron. Instead, the whole room is the cream stone I'm used to seeing at the Eyrie, with images of mythical creatures carved into the corners and ceiling. The non-fire torches make the lighting and feel of the room eerie, and I'm instantly not okay with having been unconscious in here.

What happened?

The last thing I can remember is this green-eyed chick

threatening to kill me if I exposed their secret and then grabbing my neck. I reach back and rub at the spot where she had her hand.

"Did you do it?" I ask, not feeling anything different back there.

I scan the room again, but I don't spot any mirrors or other reflective surfaces that I might use to see what's going on back there.

"It is done," she answers, but there's something about the look on her face that gives me pause.

"What happened?" I query, self-consciousness and anxiety slamming through me as I study the haunted light in her eyes.

"What did they do to you?" she asks me almost on a whisper.

I'm confused for a beat by the question. "What did who do to me?" I demand, even more alarmed as she unsteadily moves away from me. "What are you talking about? What did who do to me?" I ask again when it seems like she's about to make a break for it.

What the fuck could have happened that would have her so fucking freaked out?

"Remember what I told you." She whirls on me in warning. The fear and trauma are suddenly gone from her eyes, and they're once again hard and angry. "Stay away from Lazza and his followers. They're the only ones powerful enough to know your mark is wrong, and they can't know no matter what. It would mean the death of hundreds."

With that, she stomps out of the room through a side door I'm just now noticing and leaves me a pile of *what the fuck* in the middle of the floor. I rub at the back of my neck again, weirded out that there's something there and I still have no fucking clue what.

For some reason, I picture a big black dick inked on the

back of my neck, and I can't help but snicker. I blame the shock of everything that's happened and hope to fuck this isn't some messed up prank. Although at this point, I'd take the big black dick over the real Vow mark any day. I'm shaky as I stand up, and my borrowed shirt slips off my shoulders. I hold it in place against my chest and groan. Of course my only piece of clothing is once again in fucking tatters. It's like this world wants me to be naked all the time.

No one comes in to retrieve me, and I have no clue what to do now. Thoughts of escape float through my mind. Oddly, the fake Vow sits heavy on the back of my neck. As much as I'd love to figure out how to get out of here, it's probably not smart. The seer's warning rings in my mind again, solidifying my thoughts. If I try to run and they try to stop me, I could give myself away. I don't want to be responsible for blowing hundreds of people's cover. I also have no idea where I am and how the fuck to get out of here, so there's that too.

This bullshit tale is way too frustratingly familiar. It's like being back at the Eyrie, but with more people who look like me, and I'm rocking a tattoo now. *Fucking hell*. I sit down in one of the stone pews and stew in silence. I'm one fucked up, ragamuffin-looking gryphon shifter who can't currently shift and just went from the frying pan into the motherfucking fire. Or maybe I'm just in a bigger frying pan...I guess time will tell.

I run my tired hands over my face and feel utterly overwhelmed and exhausted. Devastation slams into me out of nowhere, and my eyes prickle with unshed tears. How is all of this happening to me? I rub my face, refusing to let any of the tears fall. I'm so fucking sick of crying and feeling helpless. I try to think through the lessons that Sutton taught me, but thinking about him makes me think of Zeph...and then Loa and how he stepped in to save her.

Then I'm forced to think about what happened between me and Zeph because of it, and all of that just pisses me off.

Lying asshole.

He's pretty much the fucking reason I'm here, and I swear on everything, if I ever see him again, I'm going to deck him so fucking hard it will break his face. I give a humorless snort. Who am I kidding? That would probably just turn him on and shatter my hand in the process. I look down at my punching hand and flex it. It's all healed up from my loss against the gryphon's face earlier when they pulled me out of the water.

Stupid, stupid, stupid me for getting caught.

I rest my forehead against the back of the pew in front of me and try to think through the *now what* that's swirling inside of my head. I have a fake mark that apparently will trick everyone as long as I keep my head down, and Ryn said he'll get me out of here. So I'll just lay low and try to figure out what the fuck to do around here until my *asshole in shining armor* can whisk me away.

Anxiety creeps in and starts to strangle that plan. Ryn will take me back to the Eyrie of the Hidden, and I can't go back there. If Zeph doesn't try to kill me, I might just try to kill him. Either way...it's a bad idea. Maybe I can convince Ryn to help me get home? I immediately dismiss that thought; Ryn has never been game for the *I'm going to leave* plan, and I don't think he's going to go out of his way to help me now.

So that means I'm back to square one. I need to either find my own way home or go track down the mysterious Ouphe that were marked on the map that's now sitting at the bottom of some lake. It's possible that they might be more on board with the *let's activate the gate and get the fuck out of here* plan, but not before I give them what they want first. And in there lies the issue. I have no clue how to do that.

A door opens quietly, but I don't even bother to lift my head to see who has come in. It's probably just a guard ready to drag me off to whatever hovel they've decided I can now occupy...now that I'm *one of them*.

Fuck my life.

I miss my bike and my freedom and...hamburgers. I'd fucking kill for a big ass burger and a pile of fries right now.

"Who are you praying to?" a warm voice asks me, and a massive body sits down in the pew on my left. A tree trunk sized leg rubs against mine, and I tense.

Shit.

Pretty sure the flower-loving, dimple-chinned male, who happens to be Lazza's little brother, is square in the category of *Lazza cronies* that I've been warned to stay away from. I peek over at him. He's about Ryn's height, which means he towers over me by at least a foot, but he's bulky like Zeph. I take in his mismatched eyes and his silky white hair, and mentally compare it with the disguise he wore earlier. Surprisingly, I prefer him like this. I shake that thought away and release an empty chuckle.

"I was praying for a hamburger the size of you and an even bigger mountain of fries. Not to any god though, there's no way those assholes exist, or I wouldn't be here right now," I tell him, turning my head away and letting the cool stone of the pew against my forehead soothe me.

"Ah," he states simply, like he actually understands what I'm saying.

The room falls quiet again. I'm not sure how long we sit in companionable silence, but I'm pulled away from my thoughts when I feel his fingertips tracing the mystery mark on the back of my neck. I tense, and his fingers pause their perusal. I should slap his hand away, but I don't. I just sit there. After a beat, he continues to trace the mark that's there. Maybe I want to see what he traces so I can better understand what's there, or maybe I just need a comforting touch in this moment, but I do and say nothing as his hand draws out the symbol now on the back of my neck.

He traces what feels like the arc of a rainbow and then moves his hand lower and traces an upside-down rainbow. It's like a circle almost, but the two sides don't connect. His fingers gently move to the middle of the two arcs where the shape he reveals feels like an eye that's missing the iris and pupil. A long vertical line comes down through the middle of it all, and a dot at the bottom is pressed into my skin by his soft touch. His hand goes still for a moment before he traces a new line slowly down my spine.

Goose bumps spring up on my arms, and for some reason, this touch feels different than the one that was just tracing symbols on my neck. I sit up and scoot away from him. My movement seems to snap him out of some kind of trance, and he clears his throat and sits up a little straighter. A flicker of apology fills his eyes, but he blinks it away and runs his mismatched gaze over my face.

"You must be tired and hungry. I'm to escort you to your new quarters and make sure you get settled in," he announces somewhat formally, and the warning the green-eyed seer spy who marked me rings in my mind again.

"Why you?" I blurt and then instantly regret it.

Nice, Falon, the goal is to stay under the radar, not piss off the royal family two seconds after you get your bullshit mark.

"I mean, it seems like a menial task that I'm sure any old guard would have been perfectly capable of," I add in an effort to seem less rude.

"True, but then you're not just any old female, now are you?" he states with a wink and then stands up.

I have no clue what the hell that's supposed to mean. My

initial instinct is that he knows somehow about my time with the Hidden or the dangerous power I've been told I hold, but that seems like an overreaction. If he knew all of that, I don't think he'd be calmly escorting me to my new house or quarters or wherever he just said he's supposed to take me. Then again, this could all be some fucked up elaborate trick, and I'm about to end up back in the dungeon on some sicko's torture table.

I guess I'm about to find out.

I stand up, my shirt gripped firmly in place at my chest, and wait for him to show me which path I'm destined to tread. He moves smoothly down the aisle, and I'm once again taken aback by how gracefully gryphons move in spite of their gargantuan size. I fall into step behind him and shield my eyes as we step out of the dimly lit chapel into the bright crystalline building.

He walks over to a door across the corridor and pushes it open. I follow him out onto a balcony, and I'm forced to jump back in surprise when enormous white wings spring from his back. Another shocked squawk escapes my mouth when my own wings shove their way out uninvited. It's like they saw what he was working with and said *hold my beer*. I teeter from the unexpected arrival of my onyx feathered appendages, and Treno reaches out to steady me. He has a goofy grin on his face as he does, and my brow furrows with annoyance.

Just what the fuck does he find so amusing?

I tie my mangled shirt halter style around my neck and waist and grunt in satisfaction when it stays put, covering everything I want. Treno gives a quick flap of his beautiful snow-white wings as he watches me, and not to be outdone, my wings give a flap of their own. I glare at them over my shoulder and send a stern mental *cut it out*. We're not three years old, and this is not the copycat game.

Treno chuckles quietly and then announces, "Follow me, flower."

With that, he leaps off the open crystal balcony, and his stunning wings work to propel him up. I look around at all the structures around me. They look like odd, naturally formed high-rises. They aren't tidy and right-angled like the cityscapes back in my world, but more organic and wild in their structure. It almost looks as though the Avowed chose skyscraper-sized crystal clusters to hollow out and then fortified the gem-like shells with iron veins and borders.

The buildings gleam and shine like diamonds under special lighting at a jewelry store. It's breathtaking and disorienting. I look down, hoping to give my retinas a slight break from the shiny onslaught, and see neat and tidy streets below. Dots of people move like little ants beneath me, and other dots fly to and from other balconies like the one I'm standing on.

I take a deep breath and then leap off my perch. Immediately, cool crisp air fills my feathers, and I swear I can feel the wind embrace me and whisper *welcome back* as it whips past. I release a sigh and relax as a sense of rightness and belonging lifts me up like the current I seamlessly begin to ride. I move higher and higher away from what I now realize is an island that the Avowed call home, into the open sky. Each flap of my wings wipes away the fear and tension that has been settling into my muscles since I flew off the balcony of the cliff castle.

My life and world may be in shambles, but in this moment, flying through the bright blue cloudless sky, *this* is where I belong. The white-winged Treno hovers on a strong current like he doesn't have a care in the world. I watch him for a moment and wonder what his deal is. Why was he out there in the Amaranthine Mountains? Why is he here now with me? It would make more sense to me if he dropped me off wherever it is they've decided I'll live and then went on with his life as the second in command of the Avowed. Or if he treated me like the prisoner I clearly am. But instead, here we are like a pair of lazy seagulls just riding the wind for who knows what reason.

Did he do this for me? Or am I just along for the ride with him?

I'm tempted to close my eyes and let myself fully relax like the dimple-chinned Altern of the Avowed currently is, but as right as the sky feels, the world is still all kinds of wrong. I take in my surroundings, and with surprise, realize that the water surrounding the island of Kestrel City isn't that of a lake like my first glimpse suggested. The island is actually positioned in the middle of a colossal and very fast-moving river. The water looks calm and peaceful all around the city, but from this height, I can see that it becomes frothy and dangerous as the rapids meet rocky outcrops further down. Beyond that, the river leaps off a cliff and dives down to places that I can't see. Lush forest lines both banks of the river, and I spot guards both in the air and on the ground far out into the distance.

This place is fortified to the teeth, and I wonder how Zeph and his Hidden rebels hope to combat such a show of force. Cloud-tipped mountains just peek over the horizon, but I can't make out their color. I also can't remember if there were other mountain ranges on the map Nadi gave me. I release a resigned huff. Until I can find another map, there's no way for me to know where I am in relation to where I need to be.

I look back down at the shining city below me and know that somewhere down there is a detailed drawing of this world, and I just need to find it. I look over at Treno, like I'm worried he can somehow hear my thoughts. He's still riding the current, pockets of air filling his wings, but his eyes are no longer closed. No, instead, those mismatched irises are watching me intently. He moves closer to me, and I tense slightly.

"Let's find somewhere quiet to land. I'd like to get to know you, maybe meet your gryphon if you're up to it...introduce you to mine?" he offers. "I'm sure you have a lot of questions."

I'm so used to Sutton and others referring to their gryphon as if they are one in the same, so it's strange to me to hear Treno talk about his like it's a beloved pet he wants to introduce me to. I run my gaze over his windswept long white hair and feel a strange warmth with just a hint of alarm. I have more in common with him than I ever did with any of the Hidden. Well, aside from Ouphe tainted Ami, that is.

The fact that he's even offering to answer any questions at all is surprising. Begrudgingly I realize I could learn a lot here if I'm allowed.

"That sounds weird and all," I say with a cheeky smile I can't help, "but I'll pass on the gryphon playdate, thanks though."

I once again remind myself to rein in the snark and not piss off team Lazza, but even if I wanted to see if our gryphons got along, Pigeon is still in a world of hurt right now. I'm not sure how long it will take for her to be up for a meet and greet, assuming that's a thing here. Judging by the way Treno's brow furrows at my refusal, I'd guess gryphon introductions *are* a thing here. I'm reminded of a bumper sticker I saw once that read "If my dog doesn't like you, I probably won't either." Is it like that with the gryphons here?

"Why?" Treno finally asks, and I smile as I visualize a female telling a male *it's not you, it's my gryphon*.

"Why what?" I query as I pull my thoughts away from all

the things a girl could blame on her gryphon. *"Ma'am, you cannot move into a Tim Hortons!"*

"But my Pigeon wants me to!"

I shake away the thought and focus on what Treno is saying.

"Why don't you want our gryphons to meet?" he repeats as he starts to circle me.

Why do I suddenly feel like I'm being hunted? And why do I suddenly like the idea of that?

"Pidge, is that you?" I ask, but nothing happens.

"It's not you, it's me," I tell him, biting back the chuckle that bubbles up my throat. "Even if I wanted to introduce you to my girl"—which I don't—"she's not available right now."

He looks even more confused now. His dark eyebrows dip down, and his blue and purple gaze moves to my ebony wings behind me and then back to my face. He opens his mouth to say something else, but I cut him off.

"She's hurt, okay? When you fuckers shot me out of the sky, you hurt her. I'm not sure how long it will take for her to recover..." *or if she will.*

I leave the last part out. I'm already vulnerable enough admitting that I can't call on Pigeon, no need to paint more of a target on my back.

Treno's heterochromia gaze fills with shock and then alarm. He darts in toward me with hummingbird like speed.

"You're hurt?" he demands, grabbing me and pulling me to him.

"Excuse you," I snap as his grabby hands fuck with all the amazing flying I'm doing.

He doesn't seem to care as his big arms manhandle me until I'm somehow cradled against his chest and we're diving back down toward Kestrel City. It all happens so fucking fast that I don't even have time to think before the wind is screaming past my face and stealing all of my pissed off objections. He strokes a hand up my back in an all too familiar way, and my wings immediately get sucked back into my back.

How the fuck do they do that?

My stomach crawls up into my chest as we fall even faster, and I'm unable to demand that he explain the whole wing spine trick. In a blink, we're landing on a balcony, and Treno is storming inside, shouting for a healer.

People scramble to get out of his way, while others dart off to procure everything he's angrily demanding. Meanwhile, I'm cursing him to the high heavens and trying to push out of this fucker's iron like hold.

Fucking strong ass manhandling douche bag.

He kicks open a set of double doors and carries me into a huge room. I stop struggling, I'm so taken by the strange beauty of it all. The walls are cream stone, but the ceiling is a massive circular crystal-topped skylight. There's a skinny tree trunk in the far left corner, and it's free of branches until it hits the ceiling, where leaf-covered appendages and vines fill in the circle of the skylight. The glow of the room is dulled with a hint of green from the leaves, and there's an oddly peaceful feel to it all.

Flower-covered vines curtain the far wall, and a large bed covered in what looks like deep purple velvet is pushed up against the vines like they're serving as a headboard. Rugs of fuzzy looking clover and moss dot the room, and there's a seating area to the left, with a tree trunk coffee table surrounded by chairs that appear to be made of gnarled tree trunks and stone, all set atop a mossy carpet.

Treno sets me down on the bed like the delicate flower he clearly thinks I am. I open my mouth to yell at him, but I'm momentarily distracted by the bed cover. Nope, not velvet, it's something *way* softer. My rubby cat instincts are immediately activated, and I have to stop myself from moaning and rolling around on the soft fabric like a fucking loon. Treno reaches down and rips my shirt down the middle with his hands.

"What the fuck do you think you're doing?" I shriek at him as I clamp the fabric ends together and spring up off the bed.

He tries to push me back in place, and I open the floodgates on my rage so it can drown out my fear. I've had enough of this shit with Zeph and Ryn. I am not going to meekly stand by while it happens again.

"If you so much as come near me with a hard-on, I swear to fuck I will bite it off. I don't need my gryphon to fight you. I have no problem with dying, and you better believe I will take you down with me," I growl at him.

He looks at me confused as I scramble away from him.

"Flower, you are in danger," he tells me, taking a step closer and then immediately freezing when I panic and almost trip on my feet to back away and maintain distance between us.

"No shit," I snap back.

"Not from me, flower," he reassures, surprise lighting up his eyes. "Your gryphon is hurt; if it's bad enough, it will kill you both. I've called for a healer. They will be here any second now."

I reel, not sure how to process what he just said. *We could die?*

"Can you reach your gryphon at all?" he asks, worry coating every syllable.

"No," I admit on a whisper. "I haven't been able to since we crashed into the lake."

"Thais piss!" Treno curses, and he reaches for me again.

I flinch, and he immediately pulls back.

"Flower, I won't hurt you. You're safe here. You'll always be cared for here."

The doors slam open, interrupting any response I might have. An elderly looking woman hobbles in, and Treno rounds on her.

"What took so long?" he barks, and I immediately feel bad for the woman.

"Hush, Altern, I have not kept you waiting long," she replies calmly, and I hold my breath, fully expecting Treno to lose his shit on her.

I'm shocked when he simply releases a deep breath and nods apologetically to the woman.

Well, shit.

"All is well, child, now tell me what has you so out of sorts." She runs her gaze over Treno like she's looking for an injury.

"It's not me, it's my..."

He doesn't finish the sentence but steps to the side to reveal...me. The woman's eyes widen with surprise. She looks me over, her aubergine gaze settling on the white-knuckled fists holding my top together. Her eyes narrow.

"What do we have here?" she asks, turning to Treno, her tone laced with venom and judgment.

"Her gryphon was damaged when we captured her. They haven't touched for at least three days," he explains, and the woman's features grow even harder with the word *capture*.

Three days? How the hell did Ryn put me out for three days?

Anger works its way through my body, and I make a mental note to stab him again the next time I see him. The elderly woman huffs and gestures toward the bed.

"Come, child, time is of the essence here."

I hesitate, looking from her to the bed to Treno.

"Yes, yes, I will sort that for you," she assures me, and

her dark purple eyes turn from me to the giant male just standing off to my right. "I see no answer, which means you have no rights here, Altern. Leave. I will come to you when I am done."

Once again, I expect Treno to tell the frail looking woman to fuck off, but he just huffs and then promptly leaves. I watch the heavy iron doors close behind him, and I'm momentarily taken aback. What kind of sorcery was that, and how the fuck can I learn how to wield it? I look back to the woman, who nods and takes me in again, her gaze somewhat softer.

"Come, child," she coaxes again, and I hesitantly move to the bed. "Disrobe, petal. It will only be me that sees you, and I need to check you over thoroughly," she instructs.

This time, it's my turn to huff and then do as she says. The destroyed fabric that once served as a shirt drops limply to the ground. The healer's breath catches, and I look down to see what's warranted her shock. Purple bruises mottle the skin of my ribs and abdomen. I have what are clearly finger mark hematomas on my shoulders and upper arms, and my left hip has a yellowish sheen to the skin covering it.

I'm shocked by the damage that I find. I haven't had time to check myself out since I woke up with Ryn in the dungeon, but I haven't been hurting or sore in anyway. There's been nothing to indicate that I'm clearly fucked up.

"Your gryphon is blocking it," the woman explains as though she can read my mind. "The fact that you aren't hurting is a good sign, but we must work fast. Lie down," she orders and then moves to the side of the bed.

I gingerly sit down and scoot to the middle of the huge bed. Now that I've seen the state of my body, the drive to be extra careful with it is at the forefront of my mind. I settle into the soft fabric of the bedding and wait for whatever she's going to do to fix me and Pigeon. Warm, rough hands settle on my stomach, and I flinch.

"Shhh, petal, just breathe, it will all be over soon."

Heat gathers underneath her touch, and then the next thing I know, I'm slamming into a wall of black, and everything is just gone.

5

I moan and arch my back to stretch. I press into a large hard body and freeze. A tan meaty arm encircles my torso, and I can feel deep measured breaths tickle the hair on the top of my head. It seems I'm the little spoon in a spoon situation I did not sign up for. My heart picks up speed in my chest, and I look around, trying to figure out where I am and what's going on. Everything is dark and has this strange fuzzy quality that I've only ever noticed in dreams.

I relax and let out a relieved breath. I'm dreaming. Fuck, it's always so weird when I'm all aware and logical in my dreams.

The body behind me stirs, and the well-muscled arm pulls me back tighter against his chest. A deep groan fills the fuzzy dark wall-less room, and my nipples and clit wake right on up. I chuckle silently, totally game for a delicious wet dream. I push my ass back into whoever's behind me and start an internal chant of "please be Charlie Hunam, please for the love of all wet dreams, be Charlie Hunam."

The breaths tickling the top of my head change, and I can tell Charlie is slowly waking up. His tan hand moves from around my waist and slowly skims down my stomach. His fingers dip into the curls at the apex of my thighs, and he groans and grinds his long hard cock against my lower back. I feel a touch of wetness at the small of my back, and I can just picture the precum dripping off of Charlie's shaft. I lick my lips and hum my approval as he dips his fingers between my now wet lips and strokes my opening softly.

I widen my thighs and arch back into him, giving him better access, and his other hand reaches around to squeeze my breast while full lips start kissing a trail from my earlobe down my neck.

"Mmmmm," he growls in my ear as he dips a long thick finger inside of me.

I whimper, wanting more.

He chuckles and pulls his finger out of me to circle my clit. I reach back to stroke the thick cock pressed between my back and his stomach, and he nips at my throat in approval. I don't know much about Charlie Hunam, but I now know the man makes quick work of a wet pussy. He tweaks my nipples with one hand, and with the other, he's spread me wide so he can play all he wants between my wet folds. He circles my clit, the revolutions picking up pace with each round. And his scratchy chin nuzzles my ear.

"Do you want my mouth on you?" he asks, moving his hand faster, the tingles building with each pass against the bundle of nerves. "Do you want my mouth on you next, drinking your sweet nectar, or would you rather I bury myself deep inside of you until you're screaming and spent?"

I giggle and then moan as my orgasm sneaks closer. Sweet nectar? Who knew Charlie said shit like that, probably picked it up in some period movie. I open my mouth to tell him to let loose some dirty Sons of Anarchy shit in my ear, but an orgasm rips through me, and I'm lost to the tingling that scatters throughout my entire body.

"Fuck me," I order, my head thrown back and my eyes shut as I revel in this perfect release.

"Spread for me, little sparrow," he commands as he moves out *from behind me and climbs on top of me instead.*

I freeze, and my lids fly open. Honey-dipped eyes glow in front of me, and black shoulder length curly hair falls forward like curtains trying to close off Zeph's face.

"What the hell? What are you doing here? Where's Charlie?" I ask, sitting up and almost head butting him.

"I'm fucking you," Zeph answers simply, his eyes narrowing. "Who the rut is Charlie?"

"My fantasy dream fuck buddy," I answer, looking around and trying to figure out why my dream self would have conjured Zeph over Charlie.

What the fuck, brain?

I mean, I guess it's better than the faceless dudes I sometimes fuck in my dreams, but I hate real life Zeph, so why him? I tilt my head in thought as I try to put it all together. I got nothing. Maybe I just needed a good hate fuck?

"You're impossible even in dreams," Zeph huffs out, and I chuckle.

"Of course I am, and you know you like it, so stop complaining and fuck me already," I snark, lying back in the bed and spreading my legs wider in invitation.

"I doubt that tongue would be so sharp with my stem buried down your throat," he grumbles.

I laugh at the word stem *and shake my head. "You'll never be lucky enough to find out."*

I call out for Charlie.

"What are you doing?" Dream Zeph demands, his golden eyes growing angry.

"Calling to see if Charlie will show up and fuck me, since you're clearly not interested." I gesture down at the stem that's not currently buried balls deep inside of me, despite my spread thighs and verbal invitation to do so.

Zeph snarls at me and then finally does what any good wet dream fantasy man is supposed to do, he thrusts deeply inside of me over and over again. I gasp and moan and encourage until he's pounding into me at a pace I love. He hits everything I need him to, inside and out, and I know the epic orgasm I'm just on the cusp of is going to have me seeing stars.

Zeph claims my lips, the tempo of our bodies slamming against one another, filling the wall-less room with my new favorite rhythm. Our kiss ends as we pant in order to fill our lungs. He pistons into me, and his lips nip at my ear.

"My mate," he declares, and I growl at him.

"Your nothing," I snap back, tilting my head to give his lips and teeth better access.

"My mate," he repeats on a snarl, his hips punctuating each word.

I push against his chest until our eyes are locked.

"Never," I seethe, reality slinking in to taint the hate fuck filled dream.

I can get on board with the carnal, but if Dream Zeph thinks he can pull that dominant bullshit in my head, he's got another thing fucking coming.

Zeph laughs, but there's not an ounce of humor in it. "Little sparrow, it's already done."

I gasp and sit up straight in the bed. I pant, desperately pulling deep gulps of air into my lungs. With wide scared eyes, I look around to find I'm in the tree room I was in before. It's night, and the space is dipped in shadows. I scrub at my face with my hands and groan. What a fucked up dream. What the hell was that all about?

A shadowed figure rises in the corner, and I squeal, terrified, and clamber back away from it. The darkness-cloaked figure steps into a sliver of moonlight to reveal Ryn. He looks alarmed. I slam a hand to my chest and glare at him.

"You scared the shit out of me!" I whisper growl at him,

my heart hammering in my chest and my breathing just on the verge of hyperventilation.

"You scared *me*!" he whisper yells back. "Why didn't you tell me you were hurt? I almost lost you, Falon," he tells me, reaching for me as I scramble out of the bed so I can round on him. I'm completely naked, but I'm so mad I don't even care right now.

"Why didn't I tell you I was hurt? You shot me out of the fucking sky, Ryn, how could I not have been hurt?" I snap at him, stepping to get into his face—more like chest because the fucker is so damn tall. That just pisses me off even more. I can't even yell and intimidate him like I want to, because he's the size of a well-muscled building.

"Exactly when was I supposed to reveal anything to you? When you choked me to the point of unconsciousness? When you spewed vague shit at me in the cell I woke up in, before you just up and disappeared? Should I have shouted it at you when I stood in front of you and your good buddy Lazza? Oh no, I got it, I should have told the psycho bitch you sent to mark me. The one who knocked me out and then ran off just as soon as I opened my eyes again."

Ryn takes little steps back as I press angrily forward. His eyes narrow and fill with frustration as I rant and spew judgment and anger at him.

"I didn't know that was you in the sky!" he growls back at me. He stops his retreat and leans toward me, his features and body language furious. "I thought you were safe back in the Eyrie. How was I supposed to know that your word means nothing?" he accuses.

"Oh fuck you. I had no choice. Maybe if you and Zeph didn't think it was perfectly fine to leave me in the dark about *everything*, I'd have known what I was flying into," I counter.

"Leave you in the dark?" Ryn questions, advancing

on me.

I take one step back before I can rein in my flight instincts and then refuse to give him anymore of my space.

"Yes, Ryn, you have me flying out here in fucking pitch black. Care to tell me what you're doing here?"

Ryn folds his thick arms over his chest, brushing against my bare breasts. Sensation zings down through my abdomen, but I refuse to be distracted by my physical reactions to him.

"That's what I thought," I snark. "You can't blind me and then get pissed when I slam into something because of it."

"We're not blinding you, Falon, what I'm doing here is complicated, and it's between me and Zeph. We're in the middle of a war, and that's all you need to know," he tells me cryptically.

"Oh, well, in that case, I'll just fly my happy ass home, like I've been trying to do since I woke up in this hell hole of a world. I don't fucking belong here in the middle of a war I don't understand or care about!" I shout at him.

Ryn moves to cover my mouth and quiet me. I slap his hand away, and we both square off.

"You belong here now, and your stubborn wings should be safe and sound in the Eyrie, waiting for me to come back!" he scolds.

"Well, that's never going to fucking happen, because even if you can get me out of this place, Zeph will kill me if you take me back." I mentally facepalm as that last little detail slips out of my mouth. There's no way I can tell Ryn everything that happened. If he knows what I am or what I'm apparently capable of, he might not help me anymore, or worse, he might just throw me to the wolves like Zeph did. Zeph said I'd be hunted and used, and that's the last fucking thing I need to go down while I'm stuck here.

"What the rut happened between you and Zeph after I

left?" Ryn demands.

I glare at him. "It's complicated and between me and Zeph," I mock, parroting the lame excuse he just gave me.

Ryn growls and throws his hands up in exasperation. "You're impossible! Why can't you just trust us and listen to what we tell you to do?"

"Why *should* I trust you?" I volley.

"Because you're..." Ryn cuts himself off, annoyance etched into every one of his features.

"I'm what?" I challenge, shoving at him, fed up with all the censorship and omissions.

"Because you're a gryphon," he finishes, but I can feel the lie in it, feel the wrongness in what's not being said. Fire burns inside of me, and in a blink, my vision changes, my size grows, and the irritated growl in my chest reverberates around the room like the snarl of a predator that's going in for the kill.

"Pigeon!" I cheer, relief and excitement crashing through me.

She towers over Ryn, pissed, and in the driver's seat of our gryphon body. I'm so fucking happy to see her, and I can't believe that my argument with Ryn shoved aside the fact that I was waking up from supposedly being healed.

"Fuck, Pigeon, I missed you so much, are you okay?" I ask, scanning our massive gryphon form for any signs of injury.

Pigeon sends me a wave of warmth and then an image of a lion dropping a heavy paw on its cub.

"Did you just gryphon speak that you want me to shut up?" I ask incredulously. *"And if anyone in this scenario is a baby, that'd be you, Pidge,"* I argue.

She sends me another image of a paw batting a cub away. The cub goes flying, and a pure wave of Pigeon's satisfaction rolls through me. I gape at the mental gryphon bitch-slap that just happened, but the snarl still rumbling out of our chest drowns out my outrage. Pigeon takes a menacing step, towering over Ryn, and I wait, fully expecting his gryphon to show up and try to put us in our place. Pigeon is fucking pissed, and I give her a mental wing five, glad to see that she's just as over this bullshit as I am.

Curiosity smashes through my gray matter when Ryn's gryphon doesn't go all caveman and rip out of his body, ready for a fight. Instead, sorrow streaks through Ryn's gray gaze before he drops it to the floor. Ryn tilts his head to the left, exposing his neck. I watch, not sure what to make of any of this. There's a hum of *that's what I thought* rippling through Pigeon, and she drops the curve of her razor sharp beak right where Ryn's neck meets his stone chiseled shoulder.

Ryn stiffens, and Pigeon releases a warning growl. I can't tell what she's doing, but it feels like Ryn is walking a fine line right now. One wrong move, and I can tell that Pigeon will rip him apart. Alarm blares through me, and I don't know what to do. Yeah, I'm pissed at Ryn, and in my mind, I'd happily rip him apart, but I don't actually want him to die. I make that clear to Pigeon, bombarding her with plenty of *activate your chill* and *what the fuck are you doing*, but she ignores me.

"I'm sorry, I don't willingly dishonor you, but there's so much more going on than you understand," Ryn whispers softly, his breath tickling the feathers of our chest.

Pigeon *really* doesn't like that answer. Fury punches me in the face, and I see stars from the mental hit. Pigeon rears us back, and in a split second, I know what she's going to do. I scream at her to stop. Beg her to understand if she kills him, it could mean our death. She's been out of it since we got here, she doesn't know the place that Ryn holds among the Avowed. I shove myself past her, fighting to reclaim every inch of our body. A screech rips out of our beak as we battle for control. Ryn looks confused and takes a few staggering steps back as my form battles between shrinking back into me and staying the rage-filled gryphon that wants to tear Ryn to shreds.

Pigeon and I don't hold back; it's all pulling hair and feathers, boob punching, and eye gouges as we both do anything and everything to take control. It's dirty and it's brutal, but neither one of us wants to let the other win. I hate that I feel her irrational pain beating in my veins. Whatever Ryn and Zeph have done feels like betrayal in its purest form, and it's fucking hard to not want to just let Pigeon end Ryn and then hunt Zeph down to do the same.

I have to peel her emotions and perceptions from mine, but it's like ripping something off that's superglued to your skin. I have no choice if I want Ryn to survive, but it's leaving me raw and bloody and hurting.

I release a scream as I shove Pigeon away with everything that I have. I find myself on all fours, every muscle I possess locked tight with the effort it takes to control my form. I look up at Ryn, my eyes shifting between the sharp gaze that Pigeon has to mine with every blink. He steps toward me, his arms outstretched like he wants to scoop me up and help, but I shake my head, a warning screech spilling out of my clenched teeth.

"Leave!" I growl out, my control slipping slightly before I clamp down on it again. Ryn's worried gaze is torn and unsure, and he doesn't move. "Leave, Ryn, or she's going to kill you," I shout at him, and he jerks like I just ran a sword through his chest. He looks horrified, then stunned. Disbelief filters into his gaze, and his hesitation pisses me off.

"Get out, or I'll let her," I bellow and feel my body start to shift as Pigeon rams against my control like a feral animal and it starts to crack.

Resignation bleeds into Ryn's stunned gray stare, and he

starts to back away. Pain rips across his face, but I'm too focused on trying to keep him alive and in one piece to care. I may not want him to die, but that doesn't mean whatever the fuck is going on is right. I keen and beg Pigeon to stop as Ryn reaches for the door, and she goes at me even harder. My senses and size change, and I know I'm seconds away from losing this battle.

"Go!" I scream, the sound a terror-filled demand.

I swear I see devastation flash through Ryn before he slips out the door. Pigeon wails furiously as he disappears, and I feel like we shatter into a million pieces of rage and hurt and betrayal. I don't know what to do about any of it. I'm locked in a battle with her, and I don't know what to do or how to console her. She burns with abandonment and drowns in wrath. Tears stream down my face as we war against each other, shifting from gryphon to woman with each breath, emotions hammering away at each other, both of us lost to it all.

I try to explain what's been going on, to help her understand as flashes of gryphons and knots and fire bombard me. It's clear that neither of us is understanding the other, and that's just feeding into even more frustration and fight for control. It hurts so fucking bad, our bones and muscles breaking and reforming over and over again, as we can't make up our mind who should lead.

A male voice shouts something from the doorway, and I swear to fuck if Ryn comes back in this room, he'll deserve whatever Pigeon wants to do to him. I scream as my shoulders pop out and the bones in my back start to rip apart. Mismatched eyes appear in front of my face. They're filled with worry and questions as they take me in. Wonder and surprise fill me, and Pigeon suddenly just stops. I gasp as my body stops shifting and then cry out as my bones snap back into the shape of me.

"What's happening?" Treno asks, pulling me into his lap, distress twitching through his body.

"Fighting," I whimper out lamely, panting and shaking from the adrenaline coursing through both Pigeon and me.

"What do you mean?" he asks, running his hands over me and then looking around the room like he expects to find an opponent hidden in the shadows or vines.

"Fighting my gryphon," I add. "She's pissed, and I can't let her kill..." I trail off on a grunt as Pigeon internally sucker punches me.

Understanding pools in Treno's gaze, but I'm too busy mentally shouting at Pigeon and trying to decipher her images to pay much attention.

"I don't know what the fuck your problem is. But you can't go around killing anything and everything that you like! I don't want to die, and going on a murder spree is only going to get us both killed!" I yell at her.

Again I'm hammered with images of gryphons, knots, fire, a phone, fabric being sewn together, and sex of the gryphon and people variety.

"I don't know what that means!" I shout at her for the thousandth time, and we both turn our backs to each other and stew in frustration.

I don't know how everything has gone so wrong in such a short amount of time, but I don't know if I can take it. It's one thing for everything on the outside to be fucked up, but this battle now between two pieces of my essence feels like the last fucking straw. Treno asks me something, but a sob shoves its way out of my chest. Out of nowhere, an army of them march their way up my throat and out my lips, arming themselves with the tears streaming down my cheeks. I slam my hands over my face, like somehow it will trap this army of devastation, but I can't hold them all back. I'm not even sure why I'm trying to anymore.

Treno wraps me up, his arms holding me tightly, as I fragment and splinter. His lips move against my ear, but I can't hear what he tells me as I bleed out my pain and frustration. There's a small voice in the back of my mind, telling me that I don't fucking know this guy and should immediately stop losing my shit all over him, but I don't have it in me to care. I'm tired of fighting alone and not understanding anything.

I don't know where to set my feet down or what to point my wings toward. I don't know what's safe or how to spot the threats. I feel fucking hopeless. I've never had to navigate that emotion before I came here, not when my parents died or my gran passed, not even back when I thought I was latent. Then I wake up in the Eyrie and learn my whole life is lies and bullshit, and all I can seem to feel anymore is helpless and...overwhelmingly hopeless.

A hand strokes from the crown of my head down to the small of my back where my hair ends. It repeats this action over and over again, gently working out the tangles, as my sobs slow. Shuddering breaths pattern my pain, and my tear reserves dry out. Everything around me falls quiet, but that hand keeps stroking down my hair as I'm held tightly against Treno. I soak in his warmth and shamelessly wrap myself in his comfort.

I sniff and ease into an empty calm, every emotion in my body purged. I drop my hands to my lap and rest my cheek against a warm shoulder. We stay like that for a while. I breathe him in. Pigeon evaluates the situation curiously while still flipping me the bird. Treno runs his hand soothingly down my head and back, and we all just exist and settle into a numb kind of peace.

"What can I do to help?" he asks me quietly after a while.

Several beats pass before I take a deep breath and

respond. "I need answers, knowledge. I need to understand as much as I can so I can try to make sense of it all. I don't want to feel lost or hopeless anymore," I confess quietly.

His hand moves softly to the small of my back and pauses there. "Very well then, let's go hunt for some answers."

I sit up, surprised by his easy response. "How?" I ask, hope and uncertainty warring inside my chest.

"We can start with the archives, see if we can find what you're looking for there. If that turns up nothing, we can check with the seers. If we have to comb the Amaranthine Mountains until we find where you woke up and search the area for clues and answers, we will. We may have to wait until the war is over, but we won't stop searching for answers until you have them," he reassures me, brushing strands of hair from my face.

My eyes bounce back and forth between his blue eye and his purple eye. I search them and then his face for any hint of deception or *just kidding*, but I don't see anything other than warmth and tenderness there.

"Just like that?" I ask, unable to help myself.

Treno's brow furrows slightly at my question, and he studies my face.

"Yes," he answers simply. He brings his hand up and skims my cheek with the back of his fingers.

"Okay," I agree, my gaze dropping to his lips momentarily before I move to get out of his lap.

He stands up with me, and I move toward the door, ready to see what we can find.

"You may want to get dressed first, flower," he calls to my back with a chuckle.

I look down and am quickly reminded that I'm completely naked.

Shit.

I whirl around and just catch Treno adjusting himself. He's in soft leather pants and a well-fitted tunic. Hunger unfurls in my gut, and I trace every line of muscle and every smooth expanse of fabric over his incredible body with needy eyes. His long white hair falls over one shoulder, and I want to push it back so no inch of his upper body is obstructed. Satisfaction grows like a seedling in my chest, and I cough and narrow my eyes at its presence.

Pigeon!

I know without a shadow of doubt that the little turkey is back to fucking with me. She may be pouting in the corner right now, but she knows nothing pisses me off like when she scrambles my hormones. You'd think the winged menace would have learned her lesson with Ryn and Zeph, but no, here we go again.

I blink and try to clear my head of the lust-spiked fog currently rolling through my mind.

"I don't have any clothes," I tell him, ignoring my heavy breasts and the zings of anticipation flickering between my thighs.

He smiles slowly. "Well, we'll have to sort that out too then, I suppose."

"Oh, you suppose?" I ask on a flirty giggle that has me mentally bitch-slapping myself and barking out a *steady, girl* as if that alone will corral my libido and force it to behave.

I scan Treno's body one more time for the memory banks and then cut that shit out. Answers, knowledge, and a plan...that's what I need to focus on. Abs, assholes, and gryphon shifters are nothing but trouble, and I'm fucking done with them.

Maybe.

Definitely.

Probably.

6

The heavy tome in my hands closes with a thunk, and I let out a sigh. Nothing in this one either. I offer a small smile at the archivist who passes by the table Treno had brought in here just for me. I slowly stand to go track down the next edition in the extensive genealogy records the Avowed have kept of their people. The only problem is, Gryphons and the Ouphe live just a skosh shy of forever. The records of their ancestry fill up several buildings on their own, and it's going to take me a while to go through the last five hundred years, which is where I started. I'm pretty sure my parents weren't more than five hundred years old, but the more I learn about Gryphons and the Ouphe, the more I'm starting to wonder.

I hike up several flights of stairs and rehome the census I just spent two days combing through. I pull out the next black bound volume on the shelf and look down, surprised to see writing. The records here so far haven't been labeled on the spines or the front covers. I imagine this place would be some anal-retentive librarian's version of a nightmare, so I'm surprised to see the gold title on the front of this one.

I'm even more surprised when I read what it is. *The Call:*

Understanding Gryphon Courtship and Mating Habits. My eyebrows dip with confusion. *How did this get here?*

I pull down the next book in the row and open the familiar all black cover. It's the volume I am looking for. I debate for a second putting the weird Gryphon dating and mating book back where I found it, but the image of some angry librarian screaming *nooooo* somewhere in the universe has me carrying it with me back to my table. Hopefully, the archivists that are always fluttering about can find its rightful place. I stack the census on top and open it up to start scanning it for my mother's, father's, or grandmother's names while I trek back to my table. I round a corner and slam into a large hard body.

"Shit, sorry!" I offer as I bounce back and check to see if the collision fucked up any of the precious books I swore to an Archivist I wouldn't damage.

"What are you doing here?" Ryn demands, and my gaze snaps up to find his stormy gray gaze looking around like he's checking to see if anyone is watching us.

No one is.

I tense, waiting to see if Pigeon is going to freak out over his sudden appearance, but she doesn't even stir. She's been all swoony over Treno and his help the past couple of weeks; it seems the puppy love she had for Ryn has officially been put to sleep. I throw up a couple mental walls just in case Pigeon is pulling a fast one and waiting for me to drop my defenses so she can rip his head off.

"How did you get in here?" Ryn demands again on an angry whisper. He grabs me by the arm and pushes me into an aisle.

"Get off me," I snarl, yanking my bicep out of his hold and putting distance between us. "Treno brought me here, you prick." I move to go around him, but Ryn steps into my way and presses me back until I'm boxed in against a shelf.

A deep growl fills the space between our chests, and I can't tell if it's his or mine.

"Watch it, Ryn. I stopped my gryphon once, I won't do it again," I threaten, as he presses in closer to me.

I don't miss the pain that his gray eyes are suddenly flecked with before he blinks and it's gone.

"Why would the Altern bring you here? Is he here right now?" he asks, anxiety coating his questions.

"No, he's been with Lazza all week. Shouldn't you know that, being that you're a commander and Lazza's third? Don't you males have some big war to plan for?" I snark.

"Falon, why would Treno bring you here?" Ryn barks quietly at me, and something in his tone makes me stop trying to press his buttons.

"Because I asked him to help me find answers, and unlike some people, he's helping me find them," I answer flatly.

"Have you?" he counters, his gaze now puzzled.

"Have I what?"

"Found any answers."

I sigh. "Not yet."

Ryn's gaze drops to my lips for a second. "Let me know if you do. Oh, and don't tell anyone you saw me here."

"Oh, so the usual then?" I snark like some peppy kid taking a drive-through order.

Ryn looks at me confused.

"Your usual," I repeat. "You know, a large serving of vague, with a side of cryptic. Hold the truth, and add a dash of annoying and arrogant. Oh, and don't worry, I didn't forget that you like it all topped off with a heavy dollop of *expect me to go along with everything*...melted, of course."

Ryn just stares at me blankly.

I roll my eyes and open my mouth to ask why the fuck I

would tell him about what I find, but out of nowhere, he's gone.

How the hell did he do that? Is this fool Batman or some shit? His scent trails away from me, and I'm tempted for a second to follow it in hopes that I can get some answers to why all the cloak-and-dagger shit in the archives. They're just books. Why would anyone care if he was here? I stand there for a second and try to think through what that was all about.

I got nothing.

I push off from the bookshelf I'm still leaning against and chalk it up to more Hidden secret bullshit. That crap never seems to end when it comes to them. I haven't seen the green-eyed spy since the day I was fake marked, and no one else other than the archivists gives me a second look. Not that I've spent much time anywhere other than here and my room. I've been doing exactly what I was told to do, which is laying low and staying as far away from Lazza and his posse as possible.

With the exception of Treno, that is. Yeah, he's Lazza's little brother, but he's as far from evil as anyone can get. That, and no one has whispered *pssst* from the bushes and told me that I'm not allowed to hang out with him. Not that I would listen even if they did.

I make my way back down to my procured table and start scanning the pages. I get about halfway through when my heart does a little leap in my chest. I blink bleariness from my eyes and lean in, tracing each familiar name with eager eyes.

Noor Solei: Born 1619, to Anik Solei and Verse Solei.
Died —.
Mated —.
See archived writings XCPU.529 recovered in the year 1927.

Noor Solei...could that be a coincidence? My mother's name and my middle name right there side by side. Gran's last name was Steward, but what if that was her married name and not her maiden name? Maybe I've been looking for the wrong combo this whole time.

I read over the two lines of information four times before a passing Archivist draws my attention.

"Excuse me." I wave at him frantically.

I push out of my chair and have to quickly bend over and catch it before the back crashes to the ground. I right it and then spin back around and wave the robed elderly male over. I don't miss his huff of irritation, and I bristle as he makes his way over to me. I mentally add this dude to the list of other workers here who aren't a fan of my taking up space. It's about a fifty-fifty split right now.

"Can you help me find this?" I ask, pointing to the line and letters mentioned next to what just might be my mother's name.

"You can submit a formal request for it, and I will pass it along to the proper channels," he monotones to me.

"You can't just point me to the right floor and shelf?" I ask, trying and failing to keep the impatience out of my voice.

"No. Even if it were that simple," he arrogantly states, "these collections are not kept in this building."

"What building are they kept in? I'd be more than happy to go there and make things easier," I offer overly sweet.

He narrows his eyes at me like I've just said something highly offensive. "The Altern has permitted you space here and decreed we assist you. That does not give you free rein to explore every archive in existence. You will put in a request, which will be reviewed by the proper authority. If approved, the writings you have requested will be brought to you."

"And how long will that take?" I ask, dropping the sugar from my tone.

"As long as it takes," he clips back.

I tilt my head in a *you just fucked with the wrong bitch* kind of way. I've been looking for clues for weeks now. I finally fucking find one, and this pompous windbag thinks it's time to put me in my place.

"Pigeon," I mentally call, sugar dripping from my tone. *"Wake up, little pidgey widgey,"* I try again when I feel her stir and then practically roll over and ignore me. I mentally tap my foot and cross my arms over my chest at her antics. *"Stop pouting, Pigeon, or I'll take away your new favorite toy,"* I threaten, calling up an image of dimple-chinned Treno and shoving it at her.

She calls my bluff.

Fine. I'll just take care of the prick myself.

I quickly run through what the potential consequences might be if I just so happen to deck the douche. But as much as I'd really love to do that right now, this is only the first clue. I need to be grateful and demure until I have everything I need, and then I'll track the fucker down and let him know exactly what I think about his arrogant indifference.

"What's your name?" I ask calmly, studying his features so I can easily recall them just in case he gives a bogus name.

"Purt," he finally tells me after eyeing me for a suspicious beat.

"Purt, I would like to submit a formal request to view these documents."

He grudgingly takes note of what I'm pointing at and then promptly spins on his heel and scurries away. Irritation simmers inside of me as I sit back down and continue scanning the pages for my father's and gran's name. It's then that it hits me. That can't be my mother, Gran's first name was

Sedora, not Anik—or maybe it was Verse that was the mother; it's hard to tell gender from these weird ass names.

I sigh and let the excitement of finding a possible clue float away. Maybe my mother's name and my middle name were common here? Once again I'm assuming my family was actually from this world. Maybe my parents never set foot in this place, and I'm just reading too far into fragmented memories and a crumbling ring. I could have been *Stargate* portalled here simply because I was in the wrong place at the wrong time.

I let those thoughts float around in my mind for a while, but even as I do, it doesn't ring true to me. Maybe it's wishful thinking, but I just can't believe this is all coincidence. The things I know...what I am...there's no way that's all by chance. I close the records I've been skimming through and sit back in my chair with a huff.

"No luck today?" a familiar deep voice asks from behind me.

Pigeon sits up like a hyper golden retriever who's so excited it can't keep its ass from wiggling. I give her the side-eye.

"Oh, now you wake up?" I observe, a heavy dose of judgment in my tone.

Pigeon sends me an image of a person batting a fly away. I snort incredulously.

"Right, because I'm the fly in this scenario."

I flash Pigeon an image of flies on shit and then flash another image of her trying to be all fangirly with Treno. *"I don't see much of a difference, do you?"* I ask her.

I can feel Pigeon's eye roll, and I shake my head. I should probably just be grateful she's talking to me at all. That's the most we've said to each other since the whole fight over Ryn. I look over my shoulder and watch Treno make his way over to me. I try not to appreciate his long stride and powerful presence, but Pigeon is flooding me with hormones. That shit forces me to appreciate dumb things like his walk or the way his hair lifts on the breeze.

Pigeon is a weirdo.

"No luck today," I admit, turning back around to face my pile of books.

He sets a hand on each side of me, leaning over to take in the books on the table.

"I thought I might have found something, but it turned out to be nothing," I go on, as Treno sneaks a deep inhale of my hair.

I don't know if he's aware that he's not so sneaky about smelling me, but I don't point it out either way. So he likes to smell me, it could be worse. He could be a raging douche bag. An image of Zeph sparks in my mind, and I'm instantly flooded with irritation.

"What's wrong?" Treno asks, apparently picking up on subtle cues of annoyance I didn't even know I was emitting.

"Nothing, just not everyone in this place is very helpful. I want answers, but I also want to punch things," I tell him on a hollow chuckle.

"Tell me who I have to kill?" he asks casually, and I laugh, not able to help myself.

I tilt my head back and stare up at him. He stares down at me, the traces of humor I expect to be in his different colored eyes absent. We stare at each other for a moment, and I find myself peculiarly aware of how easy it would be for him to just close the distance between our lips. I wonder what it would be like to upside-down Spiderman-kiss him, and then I wonder what it would be like to kiss him normally.

I pull my gaze from his and sit up.

"Well, I can't speed up the search for answers, but I can maybe help with the other thing. I have some work to do, would you like to come with me?" he asks, his smile and chin dimple on point today. "You just might get to punch some things," he adds in a promising singsong voice.

"Well, in that case..." I start, and Treno chuckles and pulls my chair out from the table.

I stand up, and he motions for me to follow him out of the archives. I'm torn for a minute about abandoning my search for information, but I've been at it all fucking day. Not to mention, if I have to deal with that Purt asshole again, I may do something that gets me banned from this place, and then I'd really be sorry. I give myself permission to take a break, for the greater good, and move to follow Treno.

7

"Where are we?" I ask as I touch down and fold my wings behind me.

Treno is already striding toward the tree line on the edge of the clearing we just landed in. I look around for the guards that accompanied us on our flight out here, but I can't spot them anywhere. Excitement courses through me as Treno smiles over his shoulder and motions for me to follow him. For a split second, I wonder if it's wise to follow anyone out into the middle of nowhere, regardless of the world you find yourself in, but Pigeon is awake and just as eager as I am. Hopefully, if this somehow goes to shit, she'll step in and rip some heads off.

I weave around large tree trunks and have to practically run to keep up with Treno and his long ass legs. Suddenly the powerful stride I was drooling over earlier isn't so cute. The trees are a different color than the ones in the forest around the Eyrie. The bark is pale and lacking the red tones I saw in the massive trees protecting the stronghold of the Hidden. Their size here is big, but nowhere near the redwood sized behemoths that gave me shelter when I was on the run from Ryn and Zeph.

Treno stops and crouches between two trees. He traces something in the dirt. I catch up to him and crouch down to see what has his gaze glittering with determination and excitement like it is. All I see is a muddy puddle.

"What is going on?" I ask on a whisper, figuring there's got to be more going on here and I just don't get it.

"Why are you whispering?" he asks me as he stands up and starts to unlace the ties of his tunic.

"I don't know, it seemed appropriate," I reply on another whisper, unable to help myself as I look around. The forest is eerily quiet, and there's a dense fog clinging to the trees in the distance. Add *the puddle of happiness* that Treno was just playing with, and I still have no fucking clue what's going on.

"Why are you taking off your clothes?" I demand when I look over and he's started in on the ties of his pants.

He chuckles. "So I have clothes to change into when we're done," he states as if it's obvious.

"Done doing what?" I demand again, exasperation now coloring my tone.

"Defending...them," he states evenly and then points to something over my shoulder.

I have the sinking suspicion that I don't want to turn around and see what the fuck he's talking about. With my luck, it will be a T-rex or something.

Surprise, you're a gryphon...oh, and you also live in Jurassic Park now! Watch out for the lizards whose necks grow!

Like some dumb kid in a horror movie, I slowly turn around and search in the direction that he's pointing. I don't see anything other than trees. I chuckle and shake my head. I can't believe I just fell for the *quick, look over there* trick. I'd bet money Treno will be all naked and tempting when I turn around. I'm about to tell him *ha ha good one* when movement in the distance makes me pause.

Four things I had mistaken as tree trunks move, one at a time, in the distance. I follow them up and up and up until my head is tilted all the way back, and I have the sinking suspicion I might shit myself.

"What in the moose fucking unicorn is that?" I ask, taking several steps back, even though whatever the hell it is isn't even close...yet.

Treno laughs and moves closer to me.

Don't look down. Don't look down, I start to chant because I'm ninety percent sure he's naked now.

"That is a Cynas," he announces casually, like the giraffe on stilts, with the long hairy boar's head and antlers, is no big deal.

"And we're going to kill it?" I question, an unsure squeak in my tone.

"Of course not," he chuckles as though I've just said something he finds adorable.

The Cynas ambles closer, moving like one of those big weird walking machines straight out of a *Star Wars* movie.

"An infestation of Mogus has been reported in the area. They like to nest in dens that Cynas have already established, and that drives the Cynas out. So we're going to stop that from happening," he tells me, his tone all heroic and proud.

"The Cynas can't just find a new place to live, or fight back?" I query as I spot more of them moving in the distance. They look like they're grazing on the tops of trees.

"No, they're very passive creatures. Cynas are useful to us for a lot of different things. Mogus are not. So today we'll chase off the Mogus so the Cynas stay here where we want them to be," he explains.

"And a Mogus is what exactly?" I ask and then follow Treno's outstretched arm again when he points to something to the side of the grazing Cynas.

I have to squint to focus on what he's showing me, and just when I make one out, the flying thing darts so fast I can't keep track of it. The Cynas bellows a sound that's somewhere between a *moo* and a *bleat,* and I cover my ears from the overwhelming volume of it. Several little creatures dive bomb the animal's head, and I realize that the Mogus Treno is talking about don't just hand an eviction notice to the Cynas whose homes they steal, they attack the Cynas and chase them off.

Well, that's just fucking rude.

"I'm going to clear the Mogus from the Cynas Prime; you clear the Mogus from his mate, which is that one..." I scan to the left until I find another Cynas trampling the forest in an effort to escape the pestering Mogus.

"And exactly how do I do that?" I query, taking another step back just to find that I've now pressed myself against Treno's warm body.

Yep, he's definitely naked.

"Well, you did say you wanted to punch things..." he answers, trailing off.

Shit. I did say that. Stupid mouth saying stupid things!

"True, but I meant a certain Archivist...not overgrown Tinkerbelle-mosquito hybrids!" I defend.

"Mogus are annoying to Cynas, but they're no threat to us, flower. If you don't want to kill them, then just do to them what they're doing to the Cynas, annoy them enough that they move on and leave our herd alone. Let your gryphon take the reins. I think you'll be surprised by how much fun you both will have."

Treno steps away from me, and the next thing I know, his gryphon is leaping into the air and flying right for the Cynas in front of me. Treno's gryphon is all white except his forelegs and beak, which are a tan-yellow. I'm mesmerized as he moves through the sky like some predatory cloud. The sun blinds me for a moment as it reflects off his feathers like it does the snow, and I swear the heavens sing down their approval as he moves through the sky. Or maybe that's just Pigeon.

As if my thought conjured the Tasmanian devil with wings, Pigeon slams mercilessly against the wall that separates us. I grab at my head as a throbbing starts just behind my eyes.

"*Doesn't that hurt you?*" I ask, my tone dripping judgment. "*What the fuck was that, Pidge?*"

She slams against me again, and I can feel her desperation and excitement to take control bleed into our limbs.

"*You're into this?*" I ask, shocked.

She flashes an image of gryphons flying together and playing, and I give an incredulous snort.

"*You just want to play paws and wings with Treno,*" I tease, like it's the gryphon equivalent of footsie.

She slams against me again, and I growl. *Hold your fucking tail feathers. Let me get undressed first so you don't shred the only pants the tailor would make for us. Trust me, we need them. Did you see the dresses?*" I ask her as I begin to unlace my top and pants. "*More like strategically placed scraps of fabric, if you ask me,*" I add, trying to hurry.

Pigeon's need courses through me, making me antsy. She's stopped trying to force control now that she knows I'm going to hand it over soon, but restlessness and adrenaline flood me all the same. I pull my shirt over my head and push my pants down before folding my clothes and setting them neatly at the base of a tree across from Treno's messy pile of fabric.

"*Okay, Pidge, I'm trusting you. Please don't get us killed or make us Mogus food.*"

I drop the wall between us and pull back in on myself as much as I can as Pigeon shoves her way in, and our body cracks and morphs until we rip apart what is me and explode into what is her. We stretch our massive wings and screech-roar our excitement over how good it feels. Being cooped up all the time sucks, and I make a mental note to incorporate more gryphon time into each day. Pigeon shoots us up into the sky, our strong wings doing exactly what they were made for.

The wind brushes through my feathers and fur as if it's saying hello and inviting us to play. Pigeon puts us into a spin, and we twist through the sky, closing the distance between clear sky and the Cynas. A terrifying moo-roar fills the air all around us, and we look over to find the other Cynas trying to impale the Mogus with its antlers.

Damn, those Mogus are really pissing it off.

Treno is so fast I can only make out a streak of white through the pine needles and leaves of the trees as he hunts down his targets. Instead of being scared off by the Cynas's war cry, it sings in Pigeon's blood. It pushes her on and makes her want to destroy the annoying little shits pestering the poor female we've been tasked with helping. I spot a dragonfly-winged fucker diving for the long-haired, boar-headed female, and Pigeon takes off like a bullet in pursuit.

Pigeon takes to the chase, fitting us through the Cynas's extensive array of antlers like we're threading a needle. She gets close enough and manages to swipe at the thing with her taloned foreleg. The Mogus goes careening out of the sky and then smashes into a tree, where it splatters like a bug on a windshield. Pigeon and I both scream in triumph like we've just achieved something epic. I laugh and encourage her as we hunt down another, and Pidge preens from my praise. She's completely in her element as we chase, kill, and dive bomb more unsuspecting Mogus.

I start humming songs from the *Top Gun* soundtrack, and Pigeon flits, flips, plummets, pitches, shoots, and swoops until we've cleared almost all the pests from around our Cynas. The last few fuckers left aren't making things easy though. These little bitches have more brains than the others did. They force us into not only chasing them but dodging the Cynas as it loses its patience and tries to take matters into its own horns.

Pigeon and I are almost nailed by its antlers and tusks a couple of times. The long brown hair covering the female Cynas's head is an obstacle too as it periodically shakes like a dog trying to get dry, and we almost get tangled up in the mangy tresses that fall down almost to her knees. Its giraffe like tail swats around as a Mogus tries to hide behind it. I look down and feel sorry for the flattened forest at the animal's feet as it steps on full round trunks and snaps them like they're toothpicks in an effort to get away from the last of her tormentors.

My full volume singing of "Danger Zone" morphs into a cheer when Pigeon rips an especially sneaky Mogus in half that we've been chasing for ten minutes.

"Only three left!" I urge.

I still haven't spotted Treno's gryphon aside from a wing or tail here and there, but his charge looks infinitely more relaxed than it did forty minutes ago, and I'm taking that as a good sign. Pigeon releases a frustrated growl as we *just* miss ripping apart another target. That growl morphs into a shriek when an antler comes out of nowhere, and we almost become gryphon jelly against a tree. She back rolls us in a way I didn't even know was possible, and the Cynas takes out a tree instead of us. The tree splinters with a loud crack, and I can't help thinking that could have been our bones.

The Mogus that just had us almost creamed goes right for the Cynas's face. Pigeon roars and dives for it, but out of nowhere the Cynas charges forward, and neither Pigeon or I are ready for just how fast the big fucker can move when it wants to. One minute we're diving, focused and ready to kick Mogus ass, and then in the next minute, we're being knocked out of the air as if we're the annoying pest worthy of being swatted.

It all happens so fast, I have no idea what even takes us down, but Pigeon tucks and rolls us into a relatively safe crash landing, well, that is until the Cynas goes in for a good trampling. The fucker is all over us before we can so much as blink. We keep our wings tucked as close to our body as we can for fear that they'll be crushed otherwise. Hooves the size of cars slam down all around us, and I feel like the Little Mermaid when Ursula is trying to fry her at the bottom of a whirlpool. We're just flapping around and screaming, trying not to become a gryphon pancake.

I spot what looks like a pocket sized little Cynas hiding under the long pelt of the massive one currently trying to kill Pigeon and me, and it all clicks. Well, shit. We have a pissed off mama on our hands. She probably doesn't care that we were trying to help; she's been fucked with by the Mogus for who knows how long, and now she's out for blood. I don't really blame her, but I also don't want to fucking die.

The Cynas above us bellows out a roar that feels like it's going to shatter our eardrums. It's so loud and angry it vibrates through my bones. I swear to fuck I can hear the *that's it* in it, and I know Pigeon and I have to figure out how to get the fuck away from her and kill the last few annoying pests so she can take a well-deserved nap or something.

There's a clear path to the baby, and Pigeon and I debate for a moment about taking it. If we hang out on the little Cynas's back, we might just make it out of this. Unfortunately, it's a bitch move neither Pigeon or I can get on board with. Another hoof slams down next to us, and I scream.

That was too fucking close.

Suddenly another option pops into my head. I flash Pigeon an image of a bull rider and then another image of a giraffe's leg. All we have to do is hold on to the leg until she stops the stompathon, and then we can try to make a break for it. We could even climb the leg and pelt until we get high enough and then push off into the air and finish off the sneaky Mogus fuckers that got us into this mess.

Pigeon sends out a wave of surprise and approval, clearly liking the plan and also revealing just how much she underestimates me. We'll be talking about that later, but for now, we scramble out of the way of angry *you fucked with the wrong bitch* hooves and time our leap. We wait for the perfect moment as if we're about to jump into a serious round of double Dutch and we need the rhythm of the two jump ropes to come around just right.

"Now!" I scream in our head, and we dive for the Cynas's ankle and hold on for dear fucking life. We dig our talons and claws in deep to secure ourselves as much as possible. I feel bad because I don't want to hurt her, but that concern disappears when it's clear she doesn't have the same reservations. She slams her foot down over and over again, and I can feel the bones in my body compress with each brutal impact with the ground.

It's the worst fucking roller coaster ride ever, and I hate rollercoasters. Panic floods me when one stomp almost dislodges us. Pigeon's fast reflexes turn our slipping into a leap higher up on the Cynas's leg. We dig into a meatier part of her appendage and ride it out.

A large brown gryphon goes streaking past us, and I feel like someone at an air show, trying to track jets as they fly by. An image of other gryphons coming to our rescue flashes in our mind, and I get the distinct impression they just announced that the cavalry's here. I *woo hoo* out my appreciation, but it sounds more like a creepy caw-moan coming out of Pigeon's mouth.

Note to self, never make that noise again.

Pigeon and I carefully climb higher on the Cynas's leg. She doesn't so much as flinch, too distracted by all the new activity around her head as the other gryphons work to finish off the last of the evil Mogus. Pidge and I get high enough off the ground that it's safe to make a leap for it, and we shove off of the angry mama Cynas just as she starts booking it in the direction of her mate.

The other gryphons back off too, and Pigeon and I waste no time getting as high up in the air as possible. Fear and adrenaline slam through our veins like a tsunami, and I watch the Cynas run way faster than an animal that size should be capable of. She meets up with her mate, and they get all nuzzly, and neither Pigeon or I can help the *awww* that bursts open inside our chest.

Pigeon and I quickly check in with each other to make sure we're okay. I praise her quick thinking and skill, and she sends me wing fives and images of us leaping to safety and not giving up. I laugh as we recount our near misses with death and compliment each other and the roles we each played ridding this Cynas of Mogus.

Warmth moves through us as a bond that's been missing, but desperately needed, starts to solidify. We're not at odds with each other in this moment, and that's rare for us. I send out a tendril of apology, and Pigeon sends me an image of her head butting against mine. I laugh and Pigeon does that funny chuffing purr sound.

"We're a pretty good team when we want to be," I point out, and the chuffing grows even louder.

We start to make our way back down to the destroyed forest floor, the rescue team now far off in the distance chasing down some stray Mogus.

I want to try and get Pigeon and me on the same page, but I'm not sure how to extend the hand of friendship. We don't see eye to eye on a lot of things, and I don't think that's going to change just because we survived this clusterfuck together. I do want us to trust each other more, because like it or not, we're stuck with each other, and we need to find a way that makes life work for both of us. Our talons and paws touch down in the dirt, and I open my mind to say exactly that to her.

A huge white gryphon slams down to the ground in front of us. Pigeon and I shield our face from the debris and dirt that flies up from the other animal's impact. Concern and worry slam into us, and images of us almost being trampled and worry and loss flood my mind. I'm not sure what the fuck is going on, but when Pigeon and I look up and our eyes lock on the blue and purple stare of the gryphon in front of us, it's like someone sparked a match and then lit our insides on fire.

A rushing burn flashes through me and Pigeon, and through the pain and shock of it, I recognize that this isn't the first time it's happened. Images of writhing on the ground after freeing Zeph in the woods streak through my mind. He said it was because of the rope I shredded, but I didn't touch some magical rope this time. The brutal and familiar feeling sends me reeling, but I can't make sense of anything when I hurt this bad.

Pigeon and I hold on to each other as we ride out the pain. We wrap our psyches in walls and defenses and hope we can come out of this like we did with Zeph and Ryn. Something niggles at the back of my mind as I think about Zeph and Ryn, but I can't grasp it through the pain. Black spots impede our vision, and my initial reaction is to fight it. I don't want to be knocked unconscious just to wake up in some new kind of nightmare. We have to stay aware, to stay alert. We have to protect ourselves.

Everything starts to get blurry and shaky. I whimper and try to fight against it. I want to stay awake. I plead with Pigeon to help me. I'm so fucking tired of being vulnerable and suffering because of it. She sends images of me wrapped up in her wings as she watches over me. Love and safety ripple through me, and it's the last thing I feel before the darkness takes me against my will, and I have no choice but to succumb to it.

8

"We found evidence of a large camp in the mountains, but all that was left was the upturned ground in the now abandoned clearing. We were unable to find a gate, and there was no sign of a lone female or a black and white gryphon," a lean male informs Zeph, who stares out past the opening in the room blankly.

"What are the Avowed doing in the Amaranthine Mountains? They've never hunted or shown much interest in the area before," Zeph observes.

The lean male doesn't answer, and it seems Zeph's question is in fact rhetorical, because he doesn't seem bothered by the silence.

"We did come across tracks for several net guns and discovered a deployed net that had washed ashore from the lake. It was impossible to tell what the tracks around the lake were from as they were old and disturbed, but we couldn't identify any sign of big game having been caught. Maybe the Avowed were training, or maybe they were looking for something. It's impossible to say at this time. Have you heard from Altern?" he asks cautiously.

"I have, just recently. He said that he's found what we need but that he has to work out a new exit plan. It seems he's bringing *back some of the others embedded with the Avowed,"* Zeph *informs him.*

"If the timetable we've set sticks, then that's probably for the best," the male responds.

Zeph gives him a nod and then a dismissive wave. The scout bows and then turns to exit the room. I lean against the wall, wondering what my subconscious is trying to tell me with this dream. Is it trying to convince me that Zeph misses me or that he's a threat?

"So you appear in the waking hours now too," Zeph rumbles, turning to lock eyes with me. "Figures you would haunt me now like the others used to," he comments, his golden stare running over me.

"Others?" I ask, my voice just above a whisper.

Zeph sighs and leans his head back against the throne he's seated in. "Yes, my mother used to come to me when I was younger. After my brother, Issak, died, I saw him for a while, and now there's you." Zeph's breath catches, and worried honey-hued eyes land on mine again. "Does this mean you're gone, little sparrow?" he asks, his voice choking on the fear that's bleeding out of it.

I step away from the wall, lured closer by his panic and my need to chase it away. "I'm alive," I reassure him, confused by what any of this is supposed to mean.

My mind is clearly fucking with me. Zeph is all hard edges and distrust. He's none of the softness and melancholy I see in front of me right now. My subconscious has painted him with all the wrong emotions.

Relief fills his exhale, and he looks away, his gaze focused on something outside that only he can see. "Will you haunt me forever?" he questions quietly.

"I hope not," I tell him. "I'm not sure what I'm supposed to make of all of this, but I'm sure these dreams will stop when I put

it all together," I add as I trace the angle of his jaw and the curl in his hair with my eyes.

I jump when out of nowhere alarms start blaring. I slam my hands over my ears and watch as Zeph shoots out of his throne, the sad and lonely male replaced by a leader ready for whatever is coming. The tall black doors to the room are shoved open, and Loa comes charging in.

"Syta, the Avowed are advancing—"

A snarl fills the room, cutting her off, and I move closer to her before I even know what I'm doing. The threatening sound is pouring out of me unchecked, and I see Loa's eyes widen with shock and fear as she turns to find me moving toward her.

"What are you doing here?" she demands, looking from me to Zeph and back again.

"Wait," Zeph calls out. "You can see her?"

Pigeon shoves forward, succumbing to the need to finish the challenge laid at Loa's feet.

I explode into talons, feathers and fur, and find us once again in the tree covered room in Kestrel City. Pigeon's large frame dwarfs the huge bed we were sleeping on, and she searches the space for Loa, a growl resonating from our chest. Bewilderment takes root in us as we scan the room and find nothing.

The iron doors slam open, and two large guards rush into the room, weapons drawn. They spot Pigeon on the bed and promptly start looking around for the threat. They look just as confused as we feel when they also turn up nothing. Pigeon turns the growl off, and suddenly all of her attention is focused on a large basket just outside our door.

I have no way of communicating that Pigeon and I just had a nightmare, so I wait for Pigeon to hand me back the reins and hope the guards put the pieces together themselves. After a minute or so, they relax.

"Sorry to burst in like that, milady, but we've been assigned to watch over you while the Syta and Altern are away," the stocky platinum blond male guard explains. "My name is Sice, and this is Dri." He motions to the tall female guard who's still palming two swords and looking around as though she doesn't quite trust that the coast is clear.

Pigeon turns to him, and I knock on her consciousness and ask for our body back so I can do things like ask him what he means. Pigeon ignores me, instead proving herself as useless as ever by turning back to the basket outside of our room. The male guard follows her focus and gives a little smile.

"These things were left for you, milady," he announces, walking over to the huge basket and picking it up. Dri grabs another basket and pulls what looks like parchment from the back of her armored vest.

They both set everything on the low tree trunk table that's at the center of all the gnarled wood and stone chairs in the right-hand corner of the room. Then they bow and leave, closing the doors behind them. Pigeon wastes no time soaring off the bed to shove the cover off the basket she's been staring longingly at. I cringe when I discover that it's filled with weird ferret-beaver looking things with long scary tusks.

Pigeon doesn't have the same qualms about them. She shoves her beak into the pile of dead animals and then throws her head back so she can scarf them down. I do my best to go to a happy place while she devours this rodent appetizer. After a couple of minutes, a thrum of happiness vibrates through me as Pigeon checks the basket for any unconsumed morsels. When she doesn't find anything, she happily recedes, and we shrink back into my form.

I release a belch that a frat boy would be impressed by and rub at my chest.

"Those things better not give us heartburn, Pidge," I scold. "Or the plague," I add, pushing the now empty basket as far away from me as I can with the tips of my nails.

I eye the other basket—not sure I even want to know what's in it—and check in on Pigeon, who appears to be settling in for a nice nap. Air fills my lungs as I inhale deeply, and I relax when I don't pick up any concerning scents. I push the covering off and smile when I find a pile of duda fruit and a huge stack of these sweet rolls that I always stole by the handful in the Eyrie.

My arms shoot up to the sky in victory, and I shove a roll into my mouth. Thank fuck the Avowed enjoy some of the same foods the Hidden do. I stuff my cheeks like a chipmunk on the cusp of hibernation and reach for the parchment.

Treasured Flower,

I hope you'll forgive my absence when you wake, but it could not be avoided. In circumstances other than war, I would be by your side. But alas, war calls, and just like you answered me, I must answer it. I won't keep you waiting long. We will finalize everything just as it should be when I return. Until then, know I am thinking of you and doing everything in my power to shorten this unfortunate separation.

Treno

I read the note a couple of times, unease settling deep in my bones.

War.

That one word alone knocks me off my axis and invites worry and uncertainty to roost in my chest. My dream interaction with Zeph slams to the forefront of my mind. The blaring alarms and Loa running in to announce that the Avowed are advancing.

Was that real?

I play back every detail in my mind, not sure how to look at any of it. I can't decipher between what could be a lucky guess based on details my subconscious picked up somewhere, or maybe I'm a fucking psychic now. The stone and tree chair is cool and hard against my back as I sit down and break open a duda fruit on the corner of the table. I slurp its delicious juice and decide to pay closer attention to all of my dreams. Maybe there's something going on there that I haven't been paying attention to.

* * *

"What do you mean, you can't find it?" I demand, irritated by Purt's curt bullshit.

I look around to see if there's another less pissy Archivist who might be more willing to help, but surprisingly, I spot no one. I've spent several weeks now on futile census scanning. Treno is still gone, and I haven't had any more interesting dreams that needed to be analyzed. Basically, I'm going a little stir crazy. I even looked for Ryn the other day, but apparently he's off with the others, not that he would have been any help with anything anyway.

"Exactly what I said," Purt states irritably, pulling me from my thoughts.

Sice clears his throat in an obvious warning. Purt glances over at the guard and receives a look that has him dropping some of his attitude.

"The writings you requested have not been located at

this time. The archivists there are looking for them, but it's not unheard of for books to get filed incorrectly or for a royal to ask to look at something without it being recorded. When it's located, it will be brought over for you," he finishes.

I eye him for a moment and then release a resigned huff and nod.

Purt hurries away, sending a worried look over his shoulder at Sice. I can't help the small chuckle that sneaks out at that. Sice and Dri are like two badass shadows. They don't say much, and half the time I forget they're there, but they have made dealing with Purt—and any other jerks over the past couple of weeks—so much more enjoyable.

I look down at my table and all the surrounding black covered records, and my heart just isn't into doing any more research today. I close the census in front of me, placing a leather bookmark where I left off, and lean back in my chair. Another letter from Treno arrived this morning, but it didn't say much other than sorry and that he'll be back as soon as he can. So pretty much the same shit that every other note has said.

I reach in my pocket and pull out one of the sweets that accompanied Treno's note this morning. I unwrap the waxy paper from around it and shove it in my mouth. It's like Werther's Originals, coffee, and a rich brownie had a baby together. It's probably the only thing keeping me sane today, and it's officially my new favorite thing to put in my mouth. I pull out two more candies from my stash and silently hand them over to Sice and Dri.

"Is this Sazo?" Dri asks me with pure awe in her tone.

I look over at the usually stoic guard and watch her look down at her palm like it houses a treasure.

"Um, I don't know," I admit, unsure how a piece of candy could evoke such an intense response.

Sice brings the wax-wrapped morsel up to his nose and breathes deeply. He gives a sigh that makes me smile because he practically goes cross-eyed with delight.

"By the moon, it is," he confirms, and the same reverence that tinged Dri's features now moves through his as well.

"What am I missing here?" I ask, feeling like an ass because I've been snacking on these goodies all morning like they were no big deal.

"Sazo is a delicacy," Sice offers, like their worshipping looks alone don't give that part of the mystery away.

Dri gives an amused snort and shakes her head at her partner's inadequate explanation. "Sazo takes years to cure and settle into its ripe flavor. The plants used to make it can take centuries to mature and fruit, and there aren't many of them left. Many farms were wiped out during the first uprising and flight. The combination of all of that makes this delicacy one of the priciest, and hardest to source, commodities.

"Well, shit," I say as I watch Sice unwrap his candy and place it reverently in his mouth.

He groans deeply, and I suddenly find myself thinking that he probably makes that noise when he comes too. Heat fills my cheeks, and I look away. Sice and Dri have been my silent homies the past couple of weeks, and the last thing I want to think about is Sice having orgasms or what he looks like when he fucks.

Damnit! Now I'm thinking about that too. I shake my head to try and clear it of the unwanted visual. If I found him attractive, it would be one thing, but I don't, and now I have all kinds of imaginary visuals that I would like to bleach from my brain.

I look over at Dri and notice that she places the Sazo in a pouch at her side.

"Going to savor that later?" I ask, grateful that she's not going to open a window into what she looks like when she's experiencing pleasure too.

"I'm going to save it for my sister's eyas. I've had the pleasure of eating Sazo when I was young; they should experience it too," she explains, a small reminiscent smile sneaking across her face.

"How many eyas does she have?" I ask, recalling the term Ryn once used to introduce me to Sutton.

"She has three," Dri answers.

"Oh, well then, have some more, you can't split just one piece with three kiddos."

I reach into the barely there dress that I'm wearing because my pants needed to be washed. The only good thing about the two strips of vertical fabric, which cover my boobs and attach to a flowy skirt, is that the seamstress sewed pockets into it like I asked. I pull out a handful of candy and hand it over to Dri and then grab another handful and give it to Sice. They both sputter and try to argue with me.

I don't have the heart to tell them that I ate twice that much this morning, not knowing this stuff was worth more than gold.

"Take it!" I insist, narrowing my eyes and pulling my hands away when Dri tries to put the treats back in my palms. "I'm serious," I argue. "Treno gave me too many, and I had no idea it was this precious. Take it and share it. Besides, I always think things taste better and are more fun when you can share them with people you care about. I know I just met you two, but I know you have friends and family. Just think of their faces when you pull this out of your pockets and hand it over."

That argument seems to do the trick, and Sice and Dri tuck their delicacies away and stop putting up a fuss.

"You're very kind," Dri starts, and I wave it off.

"It's the least I can do. Your presence alone makes Purt and some of the other archivists less dickish," I tell them, eyeing my stack of books again.

"So what do you guys do around here for fun?" I ask, looking for a solid excuse not to open up another record and pour over it for the rest of the day.

I am bored out of my fucking mind at this point. After weeks of sporadic notes from Treno, his almost daily gifts, and the long days filled with research and not much else, I feel stagnant and stuck, two things that are starting to give me an eye twitch.

"Come on, following my boring ass around all day can't be all there is to do? What's Avowed night life look like around here?" I press.

Dri gives Sice a hesitant look, and he clears his throat.

"Milady…"

I groan at the title. I've been trying to get them to cut that shit out since the day I first met them.

"For the thousandth time, you don't need to be so formal," I whine. "I know I look all milady and shit here," I admit, picking up a strand of ghost white hair and running it just under my lavender eyes. "But I'm not."

I turn to Dri.

"Don't hold out on me. There has to be better things to do around here than read genealogy volumes. Don't you guys have bars or something?" I ask.

"I don't know if the Altern would approve," she starts.

"Okay, but first of all, he's not here. And second of all, the Altern doesn't own me. I am my own woman, hear me roar," I tell her, but she just looks at me funny.

"I'll give you the rest of my Sazo," I offer in a singsong tone.

"Done," Sice announces, and I have to keep myself from

bouncing up and down and clapping like a five-year-old that's had too much sugar.

"Yaaaay!" I announce excitedly.

Dri just rolls her eyes, and Sice looks like he's not sure what to make of any of this.

I just nod my head and waggle my eyebrows at them both.

"Let's get *white girl wasted!*"

9

"To the before, the now, and the yet to come," Sice toasts merrily, his stein thunking against Dri's and then mine.

We all throw our heads back and take deep pulls of the tart liquid. I scrunch up my face, coming to terms with the fact that whatever this is doesn't get better the more you drink it. I wipe a frothy mustache from my top lip and stare at the contents of the cup, wondering how I can get out of drinking anymore of what I suspect to be fermented milk. I try not to think of what kind of animal this could have come from and instead stare longingly at the bar.

I'd bet my left nipple that there was meade somewhere behind the old wood counter. But I'm not supposed to know the things they drink in this world, and so I've kept my mouth shut. I swirl the thick off-white liquid in my stein and tell myself that I could probably convince them that we drink meade in my world and that's why I know about it. That thought helps to perk me up. That could work actually, my requesting a drink I loved back home wouldn't give anything away.

A sly smile sneaks across my face, and I look over at the

bar area again. I watch as another patron orders something and then slides a coin to the barkeep. My excitement drops, forming a rock in the middle of my stomach, or maybe that's just my body rejecting the nastiness in my stein. I don't have any money. No money…no yummy meade. Sice chugs down the rest of his drink and then belches his approval. Dri rolls her eyes and then throws her head back and does the same thing. The belch she exercises blows Sice's out of the water. I bark out a laugh, not able to contain it, when Sice looks stunned by the volume of her burp.

They both turn to me, and I try not to cringe. I drop my eyes down to the drink in my hand and then back up to make sure I'm reading their expressions correctly. Yep, they're definitely waiting for me to go.

Fuck.

Pigeon sends a thread of amusement, and I internally roll my eyes.

"I am plenty aware that I got myself into this mess, thank you very much, you unhelpful chicken wing," I snark, and Pigeon's chuffing purr fills my mind.

I slowly bring the large metal cup to my lips and quickly give myself an internal pep talk. *You got this, Falon, it's just a little milk…that's gone well past its expiration date…and probably came from a yak or something. Hold your breath and go for it. This is what I get for wanting to bond and make friends. Okay…ready set go. Crap. Go now. Their stares are filling with judgment. Don't piss off your new besties. Go. How 'bout now? Or now…*

I slam the stein down onto the tabletop.

"I can't do it. Please don't make me. It's the worst thing I've ever tasted. I'm trying to be a cool kid and look tough and shit, but if you make me drink anymore of that yak jizz, I'm going to puke!"

I throw my hands up and lean back in my chair, my surrender clear.

Sice's eyes narrow slightly, and I bristle, ready to be ejected from our newfound friendship. Dri's snickering pulls my attention away, and then the next thing I know, the two of them are guffawing and slapping each other's backs while wiping at laugh tears that are now streaming down their faces.

"You should see your face right now, milady," Dri sputters out before another fit of laughter renders her unable to communicate past chortles and squeaks.

I watch the two of them completely lose it, and I'm baffled. What the hell is so funny? I have no fucking clue, and yet their guffaws are contagious even though I'm almost positive I'm the brunt of the joke. Sice pulls out several coins and hands them to Dri as he wipes at his eyes and shakes his head.

"You were right," he cackles, "she at least tried."

I watch the exchange, even more confused.

"He bet you wouldn't even take one sip," she explains as she deposits her winnings into the pouch with her Sazo. I look from her to the drinks to a still laughing Sice, as everything clicks into place.

"It was a prank?" I ask relieved.

I'm not even pissed, I'm just so happy I'll never have to torture my tongue with that shit again.

"My taste buds will never recover," I whine and then laugh as I grab fabric from the skirt of my dress and proceed to wipe my tongue with it.

That kicks off another round of laughter, and this time I have laugh tears right alongside them.

I might be a little drunk.

"I should tell the both of you that I'm not one for holding a grudge...I cook them their favorite foods, sing songs of retribution to them, and read my grudges bedtime stories. You two have no idea the wrath you just unleashed down upon you."

I release an epic evil laugh, but its effect is ruined by the loudest, grossest tasting burp I've ever experienced in my life. I slam my hands over my mouth, too late to stop it from billowing out, and Sice's eyes widen with shock. Dri and several other patrons shoot out of their chairs and start clapping for me. My face heats up with pure, undiluted embarrassment, which only serves to spur them on as they start cheering and clapping even harder.

After a beat, I stand up, flip everyone the bird, and then curtsey. "Now someone get me something to drink that doesn't taste like upchuck," I order, and to my surprise, several people make a dash toward the bar.

I sit back down, surprised that my bossiness worked and didn't get me punched in the face. Sice grabs my half full stein and downs it, his punctuating belch even weaker than his last one. I eye him with judgment and then crack up.

"No wonder you're unmated, with burps like that," Dri teases, and Sice rolls his eyes on a chuckle.

"I am unmated because no female is worthy of me," he announces, gesturing to his body like this should be obvious.

I laugh, and he looks mock offended by it.

"I know you laugh to keep the tears from your eyes," he teases. "Alas, it is true, not even you, as beautiful as you are, could pin me down."

Dri snorts and shakes her head. "As if you'd be worthy of an Ouphe blessed!" she jeers, laughing even harder when Sice gives an indignant gasp.

"I'll have you know, I've had a few in my time," he defends, and Dri chokes on the large sip she just took from a stein handed to her by another guard.

Sice pats her back hard. A new metal cup is also set in front of me, and I turn to thank the male for getting it. He looks at me oddly and then moves to sit back down at his table. I remember Ryn telling me that *please* and *thank you* aren't a thing with Gryphons, and I make a note to flip my polite switch off for the night.

"If an Ouphe blessed even so much as looked your way, it was because of who you flapped with," Dri points out, and Sice lifts his metal cup and thunks it with hers.

"Ain't that the truth," he agrees, and they both crack up again. "It's good having friends in high places," he adds taking deep pulls of his drink.

I chuckle, enjoying the back and forth between them. I pick up my cup and sniff it before taking a hesitant sip. *Oh thank fuck, it's meade.* I release an appreciative moan that sends Sice into a choking fit and Dri into a round of giggles. I lift my stein in the direction of the guard who procured it for me and throw my head back and down the contents. The group of guards bang their metal cups on the table in approval and cheer when I hold up the empty cup victoriously.

"The good days, before the wars, when us feral boys stalked mischief and hunted danger," Sice poetically recalls as I sit back down.

"Hunted danger?" Dri teases. "More like your keepers cleared away any threats, while you boys frolicked around none the wiser, trying to bed girls and climb ranks that were already laid out for you like stepping-stones."

Sice chuckles. "Don't let Ryn or Lazza hear you say that," he jokes, and my ears perk up at the sound of familiar names. "The only one of us to earn a place is Zeph, and look what he did with it," Sice adds, and Dri immediately sobers and shushes him.

She looks around us, clearly checking to see if what was just said was overheard.

"Watch yourself, Sice. You know what just speaking his name will get you, especially now when the best of us are out there fighting," Dri warns him.

"Oh cum on the lot of 'em," Sice declares, but he drops his voice just as he was told to do. "I know who he is now, but it doesn't change who we all were growing up. You'd think we all grew in the same womb and suckled from the same tit, we were that close. Lazza, Treno, and Ryn can pretend it never happened, but we all know the truth," he grumbles quietly.

"What do you mean?" I ask, not able to curb my curiosity.

Sice and Dri both look up at me at the same time as if they had forgotten I was even there. Sice's gaze immediately takes on a guarded glint.

"Nothing at all, milady," he states, pushing out of his chair, his empty mug in hand.

Dri and I both watch him make his way to the bar in silence. She turns back to me, her stare appraising for a beat before a resolute gleam enters her eyes.

"Your connection to the Altern means it's probably right for you to know some of the history, no matter how much others may wish to bury it," she declares, taking another sip of her meade and scooting closer to me.

She runs a hand over her short cropped hair, and her deep purple eyes look around the room once before deciding we're clear. Eager interest sparks through me as Dri leans closer. I know I'm about to be let in on some grade A juicy gossip, and I'm so fucking here for it. I clear my throat and try not to look like some excited psycho as I play with the handle of my cup and wait for her to spill the tea.

"Sice's family was very affluent. He grew up rubbing

wings with the Syta's family, the Commander's family, and the family of the leader of the rebels we're currently at war with," she tells me on the faintest whisper.

I lean in slightly to hear her better and ignore the goose bumps that rise up on my arms. My white hair falls forward, curtaining us and giving us even more privacy.

"They were the best of the best of our kind. They practically bled magic and ability, and were the hope of our people after thousands of years of slavery."

Dri pauses to take a sip of her drink, her eyes far away and her tone hollow.

"The problem was that over time, very different opinions of how to lead our people into the future took root, and a crack formed in the foundation of what we were trying to build now that we were free people again. The boys were young and more interested in their urges to fight, rut, and play, but their families were quick to destroy all of that."

Loud laughter from a table in the corner catches both of our eyes, and then we settle back down into our whispers.

"Lazza and Treno's parents struck out at anyone who didn't agree with their way of thinking. No one saw it coming, but they must have been planning it for some time, because in just one night, anyone who wasn't for keeping the vow mark was either dead or imprisoned. Many were left broken, Ryn's family, and Zeph and his brother among them.

"The people for the Vow thought that would be the end of it. They expected the show of power to put people in their place, but they forgot who gryphons are in their core. Plans for retaliation simmered under the surface of the forced peace, waiting for the spark that would light everything up."

Dri stops talking suddenly like the words in her mouth burn and hurt. Unease trickles through me, and I know the next part of the story won't be sunshine and rainbows.

"Zeph's brother, Issak, wasn't the same after what happened to their parents. They would have been better off if they had been banished or something, but instead, they were forced to spend every day under the boot of the rulers who had destroyed everything they had. They weren't imprisoned. They were beaten and forced to live life like nothing had happened. Lazza, Treno, Ryn, Sice, Zeph and Issak were tutored together, trained together, took meals together.

"It was as though the leaders for the Vow thought that their bond would erase what had been done to them. Then one day, Issak tried to kill Lazza. He snapped under the weight of it all and almost ended the Syta. In response, Lazza's father had Issak publicly beaten and his wings sheared off. Our people were all forced to watch. No one was exempt from witnessing them mutilate a boy who had once been a representation of hope to our Pride...and then out of nowhere, they slit his throat."

I bring my hands up to my mouth, shocked and appalled by what she's saying. I thought it was bad when Zeph explained to me what had happened to his family, but to hear these added details...it's infinitely more horrifying.

"Zeph fought to get to Issak, to hold him as he died, and that was the spark that set everything alight. It was too much, too brutal, too close to what we had just fought to free ourselves from. Battles broke out everywhere. There were gryphons fighting to protect Zeph, to protect what his family stood for, to return the violence that had been acted out on too many families in the dead of night.

"It was chaos, and everyone lost someone that day. The rebels fled when they couldn't completely beat back the Marked. It was brothers against brothers. Families divided and fighting each other. There was never going to be a winner no matter what happened, but the Hidden were born, as were the Avowed. We've been killing each other ever since."

Dri empties her stein and stares off at nothing, her gaze haunted. I sit there, silently reeling, and try to make sense of everything she just told me.

"But why the separate sides? What Lazza's family did was wrong," I state, not making sense of why anyone could have sided with them.

Dri chuckles humorlessly.

"If it were only that simple," she states flatly. "You see, it started with people who cared more for power than for what was right or wrong, but it has morphed into more than that now. Atrocities have been meted out by both sides. Lazza and Treno's family have been systematically slaughtered. Ryn lost his sister, and the rest of his family slowly took each other out too.

"Sice's parents left to become Hidden, but he stayed here because his gryphon called to a female who refused to leave. Her family put a stop to the match because of his parents' choice, and she killed herself a couple months later. There's so much pain and anger wrapped around everyone now. There's no hope of reconciliation. There's no clear right or wrong anymore."

Dri and I both jump as three more steins slam down on the table, and Sice sits back down next to us. We jump apart, our gossip session now interrupted and over. I try to hide my irritated huff, but there's so much I want to ask about Zeph and Ryn, about this war. About Treno and the role he and his brother played. From what Dri is saying, it's as though the sons are being judged by the actions of their parents. All of them were best friends at one point—do they not have any affection or respect left for one another at all?

"Your turn to toast, milady," Sice exclaims, and I choke

on the meade I just pulled into my mouth. I cough and slap my chest.

"What do I toast to?" I ask, wracking my brain for the toasts I've heard in my life. So far they've usually been to family or to the bride and groom at a wedding. Pretty sure I've heard one about sex, but none of that is appropriate right now.

"Well, do your people have a battle cry or something you say to get a warrior's blood moving?" he asks casually, like that's something everyone should have. I try to think through things people say in the military, but I can't think of anything as Sice just stares at me expectantly. And then it hits me.

I stand up and slam my stein against his and shout, "Wakanda Forever!"

Sice and Dri both grunt, slam their own mugs against mine, and shout out the same thing. The next thing I know, the whole tavern is doing it. I chuckle, not able to help myself, and sit back down. Black Panther is the shit...no matter what world you live in.

10

I groan and stretch, the cool sheets on the bed a balm to my sweaty and fevered skin. *Fuck, I'm hungover.*

I breathe through a wave of nausea that rolls through me, internally chanting the mantra

you will not fucking puke, Falon. Pigeon flashes me an image of Sice doing the "Single Ladies" dance, and I snort-laugh.

"Shit, I did teach them that, didn't I?" I ask, trying to recall the fuzzy details. *"Damn, Sice owned it though! That dude has rhythm."*

Pigeon chuff-purrs her amusement, sending me other flashes of the dumb shit the three of us did last night. She finds particular enjoyment in the time I almost peed myself from laughing, all because Dri fell out of her chair. One minute she was sitting there, and the next, she's on the floor. At the time, it was the funniest fucking thing ever.

I groan again as I try to sit up, and my head revolts.

"Nope. That's going to be a hard pass," I announce. *"Today is going to be a lay around kind of day."*

I move to flop back down when a new basket on the tree trunk table draws my attention. I didn't hear anyone knock, let alone come in, this morning. I'm not sure what to think about the fact that someone was in here when I was dead to the world and unaware. My need to find out what's in the basket trumps my headache, and I roll myself off the bed like the lazy slug that I currently am. I caterpillar crawl my way over there, dismissing the flickers of judgment Pigeon sends my way as I do.

I pull the lid off the basket and then stare for a minute as I process the folded pile of leather in front of me. I reach in and pull out the buttery soft item at the top, and it unfolds to reveal a pair of pants. I study the front and then the back, and then pull them to my chest for a hug. Treno gifted me with a huge stack of...pants. I squeal and then put my palm to my head, because that was a really bad idea in my current state.

I pull all of the pants out of the basket so I can inspect them, and I'm surprised to see something similar to the bras that I had Tysa make for me. I'm confused for a moment about how Treno knew to have these made, but I'm distracted by what's on the bottom of the basket. A fawn leather bound book sits like a dirty little secret under the best gifts I've ever been given, and I snatch it out and immediately open it.

Noor Solei is written as clear as day, and I run my fingers over the name reverently. I doubted that there was a connection between me and this familiar named stranger before, but as I stare down at the writing in the book, I know I'm connected to it. It's too familiar not to be my mother's. I try to talk myself down and not get my hopes up just in case I'm wrong. But excitement and wonder surges through me anyway.

I look around my room, aware that I'm not supposed to have this, and hug it protectively as I make my way back to the bed. I can just picture the outraged face Purt would have if he were to see me right now with one of the precious archive books. It makes this all the better. I wrap the soft cool sheets around me and stare at what I hope are answers now sitting in my palms.

I hesitate to open it, suddenly feeling the weight of expectation sitting firmly in my grasp. These writings could say anything, and I'm not quite sure if I'm ready to find out that my parents were mass murderers or any of the other number of possibilities that could be floating inside these pages. Or worse, what if my hopes and nerves are all for nothing because Noor Solei was a lovely woman with no relation to me whatsoever?

I wonder briefly how this book is even here at all, especially since Purt was just telling me that it had gone missing. Was he fucking with me? Or was it just returned, and the powers that be approved my seeing it? That may be the easiest answer, but for whatever reason, I don't think it's the correct one.

If I have permission to see this book, why was it wrapped in makeshift bras and hidden under the pile of pants? No, I'd bet that my first instincts are right on, and I'm not supposed to have this. If that's the case, then it means Treno must have either had this book or had it found. Both possibilities open up a floodgate of questions that unfortunately he's not here to answer. It will have to wait until he's back and I can grill him.

I stroke the light brown cover again and take a deep breath. How it got here needs to be worried about later; the fact that it's here needs to be dealt with now. Pigeon gets all cozy inside of me, like she's ready for story time. I reach out to her for comfort, and she beak bumps me in my mind. I open the book, read the name Noor Solei one more time, and dive in.

It's odd to see my parents after all this time. They arrive, expecting the same wide-eyed and compliant little girl that they dropped off all those years ago, but I am not her anymore. This place has achieved what my parents hoped it would. I am not only worthy in blood, but now worthy in my manner and affectation. I have been molded to be the best of this year's Offerings, to take my place in society, a society where we are bound and have nothing. Not even our actions are our own.

This was the way for my mother, my mother's mother, and so on as far as can be remembered. But I find no comfort in knowing that. Today, I will write my truths in the book my parents gifted me. Tomorrow, I will be paraded in front of the Winged and Marked alike.

I'll be expected to ignore the desires of my other half and instead make an alliance. One that will keep the blood of my line strong, and more often than not, keep a mate under their boot. It is not our voices or our minds that matter, but what else can be expected when there is no call and no answer? Without those two, there is no truth, and everything that I am and everything that's expected of me is a lie.

I read the passage again and swallow back the despair and sense of duty that it conjures in me. There's a hopelessness in the words. I'm surprised that even in her most private thoughts, there's no hint of fight, just a resigned acceptance that this sucks and there's nothing she will do about it. I turn the page.

Tonight did not go as expected. This year's Offerings filled the room, each of us primped and styled in the most fashionable and desirable of ways. I was lucky that my parents provided me a gown. Some of the other Offerings were only given jewelry, and some not even that. I know what we were trained to do, but to be expected to stand featherless and nude, on a night like this, has a level of desperation to it that I'm surprised to find in this class of people.

I did my best to make all the expected connections. I moved in a desirable way, hinted at what I was capable of. Flashed the power of a partial shift here and there. It was all going as planned. The brightest of the Winged had their eyes on me, and I knew I would secure a good pairing and make my line proud.

Then he walked in.

His presence ate up the shadows. His power moved through the room like the threat it was. He wasn't expected, and no one still knows why he was there. Some of the Ouphe of old would claim our kind. Not usually in public and not usually as a mate, but the inevitable offspring were bestowed with power all the same. That power became a commodity. Those of us who fit in the in-between, not quite Ouphe, not quite Gryphon, learned to use the power and our gifts to our advantage. We were once outcasts among both races, but now we were sought after.

He could be here looking for a plaything or as a favor to some other guest wanting to show off their connection. Either way, I expected nothing to come of it for me. There are some Offerings who seek out a pleasure match as opposed to lineage match; I am not one of them. I kept my head down and focused on what I was there to do.

And then bright green eyes met mine, and all that I knew, all that was expected of me, was simply gone.

Goose bumps prickle my arms, and I quickly turn the page to find out what happened next.

She sings for him.

No matter how I try to silence it, ignore it, and do as I was always told to do, she still sings for him. Her first note sent me running away. My parents were livid, certain that such a rash move had ruined everything for me...for them. I wanted to tell them what happened, but a stranger wore my mother's eyes, and I couldn't speak the truth.

How could I sing for an Ouphe?

Yes, my Sire was pureblood and my mother his favorite toy, but how can someone like me sing for a pureblood? I didn't even know that was possible. I've never even heard whisperings. I was always taught that a gryphon could only call to another gryphon, and yet mine calls to him. I don't know what to do. If I answer the call, I could be following my mother's path. I would not be a disgrace to her or my Sire, given who the alliance would be with, but it's everything I vowed to never become. If I implement the techniques that I've been taught and dismiss the call, I can have what I've been allowed to want for my life.

But she sings for him, and it's not as easy as I've been taught, to ignore.

I turn the page.

Everything is crumbling around me. I thought when Awlon answered my call that it would be the end of the suffering, the longing, the hardship. I would be out from under the wing of my mother and Sire, and as unusual as my circumstances are, there was nothing that could be done for it. The Sovereign of the Dark Ouphe won't be denied, and like it or not, he's taken a half blood for a mate.

What a stupid eyas I was.

All hope that others would accept the match have quickly crumbled to ash in my heart. They want me dead. They want him dead. They want the baby inside of me dead. Tension between the Gryphons and Ouphe come closer to boiling over every day. Neither side has a firm grip on power, and things here are getting very dangerous. My lady's maid, Sedora, thinks she has found a way for us, but I'm terrified to get my hopes up. I feel certain that one day we will need to run, but I worry that once we start, we will never be able to stop. May the stars watch over us and guide us to safety.

I turn to the next page, but there's nothing. I flip through the rest of the book, but every last page after is blank. I spread the pages so I can inspect the binding, but as far as I can tell, nothing has been ripped out. There are only four entries. I read through each one of them again. I slow down, studying each syllable as if there might be some unseen meaning hidden between the words.

Four entries that explain so much and simultaneously answer so little. I can say with no sliver of doubt that this is in fact my mother. The use of my dad's name is a dead giveaway, but this is a life she *never* spoke of to me. How could this be her start in life? What happened between the last entry and the day that they died?

The car accident story Gran told me is looking less and less plausible. Ouphe and Gryphons are tough and live very long lives, it would have taken more than a car crash to have ripped them away from me. The sentence in the last entry reaches out and bites me like an angry snake.

My lady's maid, Sedora, thinks she has found a way for us.

I stare at the words *My lady's maid, Sedora*. Gran wasn't even my gran, not by blood anyway. She served my mother and then, I suppose, me when they died. The room spins, and I try to take it all in. I recall weird things that Nadi said when we sat together in the dead Ouphe city of Vedan. She said something about the last Ouphe with my kind of magic died twenty years ago. But how did she know that? My dad and mom didn't die here, so how would the people of this world know what was happening in another world?

Questions upon questions begin piling up in my head. I try to sort through them, arrange them by importance, so if the opportunity for more answers ever comes my way again, I know what to ask and search for first. My head starts throbbing again, and I lie back in the bed, my mother's journal next to me.

"Pidge, what did she mean when she said she sang for him? Do you sing for your mate when you find him?" I ask, closing my eyes and throwing my forearm over my face to help block out the light.

Pigeon sends a flash of something I can't make out and fills me with an emotion I'm not sure how to decipher. It's uncertainty laced with confusion and edged in...pride maybe. I have no idea what she's trying to say.

Tysa talked about *the call*, but at the time, the mating habits of Gryphons were about as far from my mind as could be. I thought of it as more of a dating thing. She asked him out, he said yes, the rest is history. But now, I'm wondering if there's more to it. What my mom described seemed more like an instinctual phenomenon, possibly even fated mates.

Growing up, talk of fated mates amongst wolves was more of an old wives' tale. There was talk that it could happen, but no one I knew—and no one they knew, for that matter—had ever seen it. In the pack, you chose, and once you chose, you bonded or imprinted on your mate for life. Yes, there could be an instinctual drive from your wolf to pursue another wolf, but it was still a choice.

The image of a book that probably will have some answers pops up in my mind. I remember pulling it from the shelves in the archives and reading the golden script on the cover. *The Call: Understanding Gryphon Courtship and Mating Habits*. I pulled the book into my stack to have an Archivist return it to its proper home, but I forgot about it. I'm pretty sure it's still sitting in a stack of books on my table. I take a deep breath, which turns into a huge yawn. Tomorrow I'll look through it and see what I can find.

11

"Whatever you two are doing, it isn't working," Gran growls. "She got mad at a neighbor kid and almost partially shifted. If I hadn't gone out to check on her at exactly that moment, who knows what would have happened?" she adds frantically.

"I just don't understand what's happening. She shouldn't be shifting until puberty and, Awlon, you said her marks shouldn't have shown up until then either. Why is this happening so young?" mom demands, worry soaking through every word.

"I don't know. If we were home, we could find some answers, but we're here. We're completely cut off, and I wish I could explain it all, but I can't." Dad sounds defeated, and I watch him sit heavily down into his favorite chair and put a hand over his eyes. His black hair is short now, but I like it most when it's white like mine. "Either it's our blood triggering her abilities early or something outside is doing it. I've heard of Ouphe getting their marks young if they're in a threatening environment. It's very rare, but there have been cases of it. However, Falon is safe, so that can't be the case here."

Gran crosses her arms over her chest and gives a disapproving grunt. She leans against the arm of the sofa and watches dad rub the bridge of his nose. "Will she ever really be safe?" she grumbles.

"Sedi, please don't start. We're doing the best that we can for her," mom snaps.

"You say that like it makes it all right, Noor. But what if your best is not enough? Why can you never see that?" Gran replies evenly, but she has that look in her eyes she gets when I better listen to her or else.

"And what would you have us do?" dad demands.

I flinch as though the anger in his tone is aimed at me and sink back deeper into the shadows.

"For starters, tell her the truth about herself. Tell her about what she can do. Have you never thought that the issues with the marks, the magic, and the shifting are because she doesn't understand it and therefore has no idea how to control it?"

"She's not even five yet," mom states, exasperated, throwing her hands up and sitting down on the couch like it's all just too much. She does that a lot these days.

"She's smart, Noor. You're doing wrong by that eyas by keeping her in the dark. You should be helping her understand, helping her manage it all, not stealing her marks, not binding her abilities!"

"Enough, Sedora!" dad yells, and I cover my mouth as a whimper escapes. "You have made your views plain. But Falon is not yours, and you have no say in the decisions we make."

"How dare you?" Gran seethes, pushing off the wall and stepping toward him. "I have left everything I know behind to serve this family, to protect you. I love Falon just as you do, and I won't stand by and watch you destroy who she is out of fear and selfishness. I say enough is enough. It's time she knew!"

Gran turns to walk away, her footsteps in the plush carpet heavy and mad. She moves closer to where I'm hiding in the corner, and I freeze, worried that I've been found.

"Get your hands off of me!" Gran yells at the same time mom asks, "Awlon, what are you doing?"

I stare, frozen in shock as dad shoots out of his chair and grabs Gran from behind.

"I bind you, Sedora, steward to my family. I bind your tongue from speaking about who and what Falon is. I bind your animal from ever revealing itself again. I bind you to us so that you may never leave. I mark you and bind you; as it is spoken, it is so.

"Savo truss farin tamod quass. Mayhara elod tamod leerah. Rukke seeri wain voru halturenna."

"Awlon, no!" mom commands as she tries and fails to pull dad's arms from around Gran. Gran is crying as dad uses the power words he tells me I should never use. I step out of my hiding spot and run to Gran. I try to pull at dad's hands and scream for him to stop like mommy is. But he doesn't stop.

"You're hurting my gran!" *I scream as my own tears spill down my cheeks.*

Gran gasps like I hurt her, and I let go, worried that I have. Dad steps away from her, and she looks at me while mom and dad fight. I don't understand what I see in Gran's eyes, but it makes me so sad. I open my arms like she does for me when my heart feels too much and I need cuddles. But it just makes Gran look sadder. Maybe if I draw her a picture, she'll feel happy. She always likes my pictures, especially when I draw the sky.

I turn to go get my colors for Gran, but dad calls me. He has that mad voice again, and I don't want to turn around. He speaks more power words, and I'm suddenly so tired. I drop to the ground so I can lie down. I look over, surprised to see Gran standing next to me. Why is she crying? I'm so tired. I'll have to ask her when I wake up.

. . .

I jerk awake with a gasp. Sorrow, confusion, and anger surge through me like a tidal wave, and I roll over to my side and pull my arms and legs into me.

What the fuck did my dad do?

I can't reconcile the happy lime green eyes of my memories with what I just saw. How could he? I'm not sure if I'm asking on behalf of my gran or me. I wipe at my wet cheeks and wonder why the flashes are surfacing now. I think back to the crumbling of the ring on my finger. Is that really it though? Could one ring change how I look, what I can do, what I can remember?

Pain lances through me as I'm once again reminded of how little I know about myself. My gran was right, my parents should have told me the truth; instead, they took things from me. Memories, abilities...more...I know there's more, but I can't pin down exactly what. Even now, this fog that's always been in my head is still thick and heavy.

They did this to me.

I fold in on myself as much as possible and try to understand the *why* of it all. No matter how hard I try though, I can't. Anger slowly stalks through my body. So far, I've aimed all my frustration and vitriol at my gran, but she didn't do this.

She didn't do this.

I repeat the truth again and instantly feel even more awful. I've been so pissed at her this whole time I've been here, and none of this was her fault. It's clear that even in death, she was trying to show me the truth. She was trying to help me understand.

"I'm so sorry, Gran," I lament, and then I let the floodgates open. Everything she did was out of love...to protect me...even from my parents.

I shove away thoughts of my dad and my mother. I don't know how to deal with them or with what they did. I don't even know what in my head I can trust and what I can't. I love them, I have my whole life. I've always remembered them as loving and attentive, but right now, hate and anger at the thought of them overwhelms everything else. Is my whole childhood some brainwashed inception? I'm so pissed off right now, and I have no idea what to do about it. How do you yell at dead people? How do you get them to understand that they fucked up?

I laugh hollowly at my stupid questions. They're gone. They have been since I was five. What do they care when it comes to the consequences of their actions? I think of Treno's parents and the war their actions caused. We're all just suffering and trying to make the best of what's been done to us. Loss and frustration simmer inside of me, and I wish there was something I could do to get rid of it.

Suddenly, lying here, fetal and fuming, feels pathetic. I push out of bed and stomp into the bathroom where I angrily bathe and clean up. I march over to my new pants and bras and get dressed, irritated even more that the thoughtful gift Treno gave me doesn't sweeten the sourness I feel saturating my every cell right now. I throw a linen shirt on over my makeshift bra and pick up the book that I set on the table last night and throw it across the room.

The pages make a fluttering sound as they sail through the air, and then a thunk fills the room as my mother's journal slams against the tree trunk growing in the corner. It falls to the ground and spreads open to reveal a blank page.

"Fuck you," I snap at the book, and then I pull the doors open and walk out of the room, unsure of what to do.

Dri and Sice aren't standing sentry outside of the doors like I expect, and I pause, even more confused by the fact that it seems I was left alone. Irritation and aggression feel like static in my limbs, and I can practically feel Pigeon ruffle her feathers inside of me. Both of us are itching to rage, to hunt, to tear something apart. She flashes an image of a Cynas and Mogus, and I snort and shake my head as I wander through the crystalline building I've been calling home since I got here.

"*I don't think we'll get lucky enough to find another Mogus infestation this soon, but maybe we can find lessons like Sutton had in the Eyrie,*" I tell her.

Pigeon rolls her eyes and gives an irritated squawk that makes me cringe.

"*I didn't mean that you didn't know how to hunt or fight on your own, Pidge. Don't take it personally. I'm just saying that I don't know how to hunt or fight on my own,*" I explain.

She flashes me Mr. Miyagi. I stop mid step and stare at the famous character from *Karate Kid* for a minute.

"*You want me to wax something?*" I tease, not able to keep myself from ruffling her feathers. What can I say, I'm a petty bitch who won't forget all the fucked up situations she didn't help with when we first got here.

Pigeon snaps her beak at me in our mind, and I laugh at the impotent threat.

"*You do know that ripping my head off is the same as ripping your own head off, right? I don't even think it's physically possible, so now you just look like a dodo bird.*"

Pigeon starts to angrily recede inside of me, and I roll my eyes.

"*You're very sensitive for a turkey that likes to leave me hanging on the regular, Pidge. You still expected me to talk to you after the whole Zeph and Ryn 'cleansing' thing, and the 'let's not clue Falon in on anything' bullshit you also like to pull. So don't play the pout card with me,*" I scold, and I feel her huff.

She doesn't go anywhere, so I take that as a good sign.

"*Okay, you want to Miyagi me—does that mean you would like to teach me to hunt and fight?*" I ask in a voice normally reserved for little kids.

Pigeon shoots me a look that clearly expresses she's not impressed by my placating tone. This time I let out a huff.

"Fine. We'll do it your way, but, Pigeon, I need to learn how to fight in my form too, and no offense, how are you going to help with that?" I ask.

Pigeon gives me an indignant snort and sends me an image of a wing patting me on the head. I recycle the unimpressed look she previously gave me and sling it back at her. I watch in my mind as a feather is pressed against my lips like it's a finger meant to shush me, and then Pigeon signals for me to follow her. I can't help but chuckle at the cheekiness of it all, while simultaneously being annoyed.

Patrick Swayze's voice fills my mind, saying, "Nobody puts Baby in a corner." Only I mentally edit it to say, "Nobody shushes Falon with a feather."

Pigeon and I both chuckle, and she flashes me the sky and a clearing. I look around at the mostly empty halls and wonder if I'm allowed to just leave. I shake my head at that thought, because I'm a grown ass woman and should just go wherever the fuck I want to go. I turn the corner and notice a guard standing solitary in the corner.

"Hello," I greet him and move in his direction. "I'm just going to go find some space to...uh...exercise. Just wanted to let you know, in case anyone needs me for anything," I tell him, waving awkwardly and stepping away from him when he looks at me like he could give two fucks what I'm going to do.

I continue to back away, shooting a thumbs up in the direction of the guard who is now ignoring me, and aim a glare at Pigeon when she cracks up inside of me. I'm pretty sure she's mocking my *I'm a grown ass woman* thoughts from before and...well, frankly...it's rude.

"I probably just saved us from getting shot out of the sky by

one of those net thingies. Remember how lovely that felt," I point out smugly, making my way to the closest balcony.

Pigeon shoots me an image of Dr. Evil from Austin Powers saying, *"Riiiight."*

"You know, I never thought I would say this, but I liked you better when you were quiet," I tell her, opening the door that leads outside and calling on my wings.

She snickers, but I ignore it as I leap off the balcony in search of a good place for us to figure our shit out and tap into our inner badass.

This should be interesting.

* * *

"You want me to what?" I ask, the panic and doubt ringing clear in my voice.

Pigeon replays the action movie she just mistook for real life in my mind. I watch as she dives out of the sky until we're only a couple feet off of the ground. She slows us slightly and then we shift into me. I start running, not missing a beat in order to keep our pace. Then bend over to snatch a twig from the ground, and when I straighten up, we shift back into Pigeon and climb high into the sky.

Internally I stare at her, my look communicating just what I think of this birdbrained plan.

"There are easier ways to kill me, you know," I declare, folding my hands over my chest.

She flashes me the image of us successfully completing the last challenge that I declared was impossible.

"I am aware that I have said that before, but it doesn't make it any less true," I point out.

Pigeon proceeds to bombard me with a slideshow of all the things we've accomplished in the three days we've been coming out here. We spent the first day on the baby steps.

We worked on partial shifting in my form and in Pigeon's. I can now shift and call on talons, Pigeon's eyes, a soft downy coat of fur from the waist down—which I'm still not sure how I feel about—and I can work up a growl that would make any mama lion proud.

Pigeon also gave me a thorough flight lesson. Which, surprisingly, has helped to make everything that's happened since go much more smoothly.

A ripple of smugness breaches my thoughts.

"Okay, fine, maybe it wasn't that surprising since you specifically flashed me how important it would be, but you are a dramatic little bird, so forgive me for not falling hook, line and sinker for everything you say," I tell her. *"Are you sure this next task isn't like the one you created about keeping my wings clean?"* I ask incredulously.

Pigeon snickers.

"Pigeon!" I warn, not interested in falling for another prank.

On day two, we spent most of the day jumping off an outcropping of rock on the side of the waterfall. I would jump off as me and then mid fall, we would shift into Pidge. We acquired an audience around noon, or at least that's when Dri and Sice started cheering and rating my form, as my naked ass leapt flying squirrel style out over the edge of the water.

Turns out, they'd been following me and Pidge around the whole time, laughing their asses off. I look around the clearing now. I know they're here, and yet I couldn't tell you where if my life depended on it. Pidge had a conniption fit when I asked them for help though. She went all flashy and angry and then made me promise to trust her.

That's when she took things to a whole other level. Here Pigeon and I were, riding high on our perfect execution of a bunch of death-defying shit, when she flashed me the next lesson. She insisted that it was vitally important to clean my wings each time I partially shifted...with my tongue. I, being the dumbass that I am, trusted her. I was about four feather licks in when she finally admitted she was fucking with me.

"It took me the rest of the day to get the feather fuzz out of my mouth!" I shout at her when the image my thoughts conjure up sends her into another fit of gryphon purr-chuff giggles.

"Just for that, I'm going to put a stop to the explicit fantasies I've been allowing to play out in our head for the last three nights. You know, the ones about us with Treno...and Ryn. I was on board with your dirty little daydreams because I knew it made your kinky ass happy, but tonight...tonight I'm going to replay every detail of Downton Abbey *that I can remember. How do you like them apples?"* I threaten.

I get the distinct impression—from Pigeon's new fit of gryphon giggles—that she might be calling me out on my insinuation that *she* was the only one enjoying those fantasies. I say nothing, and she gives me a condescending mental *"mmm-hhmmmmm."*

"Anyway, that's not the point," I defend. *"I want you to swear on all of your dirty gryphon porn hopes that this next challenge is serious,"* I demand.

Pigeon sends me an image of her crossing over her heart with her talons and then raising them to the side like she's being sworn in as a witness or something. I exhale a resigned breath and pinch my temples.

Fuck, this is going to hurt.

Pigeon takes over, and we rise easily into the sky. She circles the clearing we've been working in and then drops. As we dive, she replays the sequence that we're trying to accomplish, and I concentrate on each step. Our wings shoot out at our sides, and we activate our feathered flaps and slow. I shove forward until I own our body again. My feet hit the ground, and a cheer roars inside of me when I don't immediately biff it.

I get exactly three strides in...and then biff it. I smash into the ground hard, but my feet don't get the *awww fuck* memo, because they keep going. The next thing I know, I've folded myself ass over head, and I'm pretty sure I need to get very comfortable with this position, because I'll never be able to move again. I grunt, stuck, as the dirt and debris settle around me.

"*Sandra Bullock made this bobcat-pretzel thing look a hell of a lot sexier in* Two Weeks Notice," I observe as Pigeon proceeds to lose her shit.

She just keeps showing me images of a two-by-four flipping end over end across the ground, as if that's supposed to mean something to me.

Fucking chirpy little parakeet.

Just when I'm on the verge of shouting *I've fallen and I can't get up* and assume things can't get any worse, a round of clapping starts up inside the trees to my right.

Just kill me now.

12

The clapping starts to sound louder, and I roll my eyes. Pigeon and I are giving Sice and Dri enough material for them to start a long and prosperous career in standup comedy. They're the life of the tavern now, or so they say, regaling the patrons with stories of my epic fails and all the dumb shit Pigeon makes me do. I stay firmly planted in the pool of mortification I'm currently lounging in and wait for one of them to come help me up.

"Just when I think you can't get any more interesting, Falon, you do something that proves just how wrong I was," Ryn states, humor and amusement leaking out of his tone in spite of his obvious efforts to stem them.

I freeze, shocked that he's here, and try to keep my cool despite my current predicament.

"That'll teach you to underestimate me," I chirp, rolling my eyes at him and at myself, because fucking hell, I really can't move. My legs are wedged somehow in front of me, and I'm stuck in a fucked up backbend from hell.

I spit to clear my mouth of some of the dirt that's invaded and try to think through how the fuck to get out of this.

"A little help here, Pidge?" I order.

She ignores me, focused fully on Ryn as he slowly moves closer to us.

"What are you doing here?" I ask on a grunt as I attempt to get my arms underneath me so I can de-pretzel myself. "Aren't you supposed to be off fighting a war? Remind me which side you're on though, because I still can't tell," I snark.

Ryn snorts out a laugh, and his leather boots come into my line of sight. He doesn't immediately move to help me, and I growl.

This fucker is going to make me beg, I just know it.

"So what are you up to out here, unprotected and alone?" Ryn asks, and there's a hint of something I can't quite put my finger on in his tone.

Concern? Incredulity? Relief?

"Oh you know, just falling for my gryphon's bullshit," I answer casually and spit a little more dirt out of my mouth.

"If I touch you, will your gryphon take issue with it?" he queries, a slight rise in his voice on the word *gryphon*, betraying the confidence he's currently exuding.

I check in with Pigeon to gauge how she's feeling right now. The erotic fantasies must have worked like a magic eraser, because I sense none of the rage that was there when she tried to kill him before. If I didn't know better, I'd suspect that she's kicking back with a bowl of popcorn, eager to see how things are going to unfold.

"She said she'd make an exception just this once," I lie, apparently not very well either, because Ryn chuckles like he can see right through it.

A zing of warmth shoots right through me as Ryn grabs me by the waist and picks me up. He manhandles me like I weigh nothing and sets me on my feet in a move that shouldn't be so easy for him and so hard for me.

I push my mess of hair out of my eyes, and Ryn's holding a small canteen out to me. I eye it for a second and then him before reaching out for it. I take a deep pull, intending to swish and wash my mouth out, but it's not water like I thought it was. Sweetness explodes in my mouth, and I immediately choke on it, surprised by the flavor when I expected there to be none.

I bend over and spit the saccharine-laced liquid out of my mouth. I then proceed to attempt to hack up both of my lungs.

"Cum on a tree sprite, Falon, don't try to kill yourself so soon after I just rescued you," he teases, hitting my back firmly to help clear my lungs of fluid.

I finally get a hold of myself and manage to straighten up. I take another pull from the canteen still in my hands, this time expecting the explosion of flavor. I clean my mouth out and then drink a good amount down.

"Careful," Ryn warns, "Toag nectar is used when a soldier needs energy in a long battle. There's no telling what it might do to your more delicate sensibilities."

I snort. "I'm tough, don't you worry your pretty little head about me, *Altern*," I challenge, using the title he has amongst the Hidden.

His eyes narrow slightly, but he doesn't say anything.

I let loose an epic belch, and Ryn's eyes widen in surprise. I smirk at him.

"What? That would have gotten me applause at the tavern," I tell him, proud of the man burp.

Where's Sice when you need him?

Ryn pinches his temples like this information exasperates him. "You're supposed to be laying low until I can get us out of here, Falon. Not drinking in taverns with..." he trails off. "Who in the rut took you drinking?" he demands to know on a tired sigh.

"I am laying low," I snap. "And I was with the guards Treno assigned, so I was fine,"

"Treno didn't assign anything, I did, and where are those guards now, Falon?" he asks, looking around like he expects them to step out of the woods.

I do the same thing. They were here earlier.

I shrug, confused by where they could have gone and by Ryn assigning them to me and not Treno.

"We should go. All of Kestrel is practically looking for you, at this point," he tells me casually as he places a hand at the small of my back in an effort to herd me.

I realize in that moment, with his warm hand against my bare skin, that I'm butt ass naked. To his credit, Ryn's eyes haven't dipped below mine this whole time. Then again, maybe he got an eyeful when he found me ass over face on the ground. I turn to the tree whose roots are protecting my clothes.

"Why are they looking for me?" I ask, perplexed. "I've been coming out here for days with no one being bothered by it. Sice and Dri are always close by; they're sneaky fuckers, by the way," I point out, impressed and equally jealous of their mad sneaking skills. "Anyway, why would anyone care where I am now?" I query, hastily moving in the direction of my clothes.

"Because Treno wants to see you, and what the little Altern wants, the Altern gets," Ryn mocks.

"So he's okay then?" I ask, unable to stop the relief in my voice from shining through.

Ryn's eyes grow hard, and he studies me, not bothering to answer.

I bend over to pick up my newly gifted makeshift bra, and Ryn grunts.

"Well, at least your sneaky guards managed to deliver the things they were told to," Ryn states irritably.

I stare at him for a second, the soft leather of the garment I assumed Treno gave me clutched in my hand, and it clicks.

"It was you?" I state on a shocked whisper.

I give a hollow laugh and stare at the bra in my palms. Ryn is the only one to ever see me wearing this. How could I have not made that connection earlier?

Ryn's eyebrows dip with confusion. "Of course it was me. Who else could it have been?" he asks incredulously.

I shake my head and study his face, trying to understand why Ryn would have given me all of these things.

"Treno," I state simply, and I watch as Ryn's gray gaze fills with fire.

He steps toward me until our bodies are flush with one another.

"And why would *Treno* give you any of those gifts?" he asks, his voice angry but even, like it's the calm before the storm.

"Why would *you*?" I challenge instead of answering.

A slight flush works its way up Ryn's neck, and its appearance makes me infinitely more curious for an answer to my question. Ryn's lips press together like he's battling to keep the answer inside.

"Why?" I ask again, my gaze bouncing back and forth between his storm cloud stare.

"Because it's what females of your stature expect in life. I was helping you to grow accustomed to that."

I growl at him, unable to stop the sound of pure displeasure from crawling up my throat. I can practically taste the lie, and it pisses me off. I step back, dropping the bra from my hands and walk away from him.

"Where are you going?" he demands.

"Pigeon and I have work to do still," I state flatly. "We'll come back when we're done, just like we have the entire time you and Treno have been gone," I add flippantly.

I internally tap Pigeon and circle my finger to indicate it's time to mount up.

"Did you not hear me when I said that the whole island is looking for you?"

"Let them!" I shout out, interrupting him. "Feel free to fly your annoying ass back there and tell them I'll be along when Pigeon and I are good and fucking ready to return."

Pigeon wing fives me, and I shake out my muscles, ready to eat dirt however many times it takes for us to get this right. I sprint toward the trees, initiating a move Pigeon and I mastered earlier where I run, jump up in the air as high as I can, and we shift and fly away. My feet pound hard against the grass covered ground as I pick up speed.

"Falon!" Ryn shouts at me, a warning in his tone, but I ignore it and leap up into the sun-kissed sky. Pigeon pushes forward, ready to take the reins and set up the next challenge again, but arms circle around my hips, and I'm side tackled like I'm a quarterback being sacked.

Motherfucker.

Pigeon seems more amused by this than I'd expect her to be, but I'm fucking pissed. Who the fuck does Ryn think he is? I'm slammed to the ground, but I rotate onto my back and slash across Ryn's chest with the sharp talons now tipping the fingers of my hand. Ryn hisses and rolls off of me, pushing to his feet.

He looks down at his chest and touches the blood welling up from the scratches I just carved there. He looks from his blood tinged fingertips to me, surprise and something else akin to excitement in his eyes. A hum of eagerness floats through me too, and I work to not roll my eyes at its presence.

Someone save me from these weird ass birds and the strange shit that turns them on.

"So you haven't just been out here rolling around naked in the dirt," Ryn snidely observes, his hand dropping to his side.

Pigeon sends a warning to me to watch how his muscles are tensing despite the smooth tone of his voice. I wave her away with a *thank you* and eye exactly that. Ryn charges me precisely like Pigeon warned me he would. I move to the side, avoiding the tackle, and call on my wings. I dive back, forcing my wings to support me, and partially shift my lower body into the powerful big cat legs that Pigeon has. I kick out mercilessly at Ryn, and he goes flying.

I shift all parts back to me and put my wings away as Ryn flies through the air away from me. I fully expect him to go crashing into the ground, and I prepare my snide remark about *look who's playing in the dirt now,* but Ryn calls on his own wings and rights himself. He plants his feet lightly on the ground and smiles at me.

"Good to see you're taking things seriously now," he declares, and I glare at the dig barely hidden in the compliment.

"Good to see you're the same ol' asshole you've always been. Here I was thinking you might just turn out to be a nice guy. Guess I'll rescind the pity fuck I might have thrown your way."

Ryn chuckles, but his eyes flash with anger. His wings give a flap, and my wings pop out of my back like eager puppies who were just promised a treat.

Fucking hell.

Ryn's smile turns devilish like he just proved some point, and that irritates the shit out of me. I pull my wings into my back and scold them for being overeager.

"Ohh, you got my wings to open," I mock with faux

surprise. "Too bad for you my thighs don't work like that," I add with a glare.

Ryn takes a step closer to me and laughs, but once again the humor doesn't meet his eyes. "You want to see the magic I can work between your thighs, Falon? Is that it?"

I snort. "Na, I think Treno might be a better fit there."

Ryn leaps for me as Treno's name leaves my lips, and I leap back to try and avoid him. This time, I'm not fast enough. I make a mental note to still pay attention to body language while shit talking. Pigeon gives me an approving nod and then strolls back to her imaginary bowl of popcorn and her gryphon sized Lazy Boy.

Ryn digs his fingers into my sides, and I wait for the pain to sink in, figuring he's going to use talons on me like I did him. Instead, I get all squirmy when I realize that he's tickling me instead.

What in the actual fuck? Who tickles someone that's trying to beat the shit out of them?

I growl, annoyed by the fact that he's clearly not taking this seriously. I wiggle away from him slightly and slam an elbow down on his neck. A threatening rumble moves from his body to mine, and he reaches up to pin my hands down. I shift until my fingers are razor sharp again and call on my wings. I use my wings to help push me off of my back and start swiping at Ryn.

He may be up for a tickle party, but I want blood and retribution.

Ryn snarls at me, or rather his gryphon snarls at me, when I claw lines up his neck and cheek. Pigeon comes screaming forward, and I can practically hear her saying *oh no he didn't* while she pulls off imaginary earrings and readies herself for a brawl.

Ryn blinks, and his gryphon's eyes disappear. I shove Pigeon back with an *I got this* and use my wings to shove

Ryn off of me. I leap up and then fly backward, keeping him from tackling me again. He jumps up in the air to even the playing field. I turn and make a wing sprint in the direction of Kestrel. Ryn grabs me by the ankle before I can even get a yard away. He drops like a sack of boulders, back down to the ground, pulling me with him as he does. I screech and kick to try and break his hold, but he's too fucking strong.

"Where do you think you're going?" he grunts out as he continues to muscle me out of the air. My wings flap furiously as I try to keep that from happening. I inadvertently kick up wind, dust and other forest debris as I try to get away.

"Thought I'd look in on Treno," I grunt back.

Satisfaction flares inside of me when Ryn reacts the way I knew he would. He gets pissed. Now that I know Treno is a sore spot for him, I won't be able to stop picking at it.

"You think that Marked prick cares for you?" he challenges, triumph flashing through his gray eyes as he manages to finally pull me to the ground.

I try to leap away, but he's too fast. He grabs me by the waist and pulls me under him.

"You think he'll ever care more for you than he does power?"

I land blow after blow against Ryn's chest, arms, face, neck.

"He's not capable of it, Falon," he warns, ignoring my assault like it's nothing.

Pigeon is practically clapping inside of my head, and I'm confused by it until she slams me with desire.

"Damnit, Pigeon, this is not foreplay," I yell at her, but she ignores me and immediately starts bombarding me with flashes of gryphon porn.

"If you're trying to turn me off, it's working!" I yell at her, and the flashes immediately stop.

I study Pigeon for a beat. *"One minute you want to rip him apart, now you want me to fuck him?"* I ask, bewildered by the one-eighty.

"You have all you need, Falon, you just don't want to admit it. You like the game too much," Ryn tells me, pulling my focus from Pigeon back to him.

"What?" I ask incredulously.

"You like being chased. You like the hunt. You especially like being caught," he declares, finally pinning my hands on each side of my head.

He leans down in one quick motion and runs the tip of his nose in a circle around my diamond hard nipple. Fire explodes low in my abdomen, and a moan sneaks out of my lips. My legs spread open in invitation, and Ryn chuckles.

"So much for your thighs not working like that," he teases, and I growl at him.

Shit. I'm pretty much never going to live that down now.

"You want to talk, or you want to continue showing me how much I like being caught?" I snap up at him.

Ryn brings his eyes level with mine and settles himself between my thighs. I like the weight of him there, and Pigeon sends me her eager agreement.

"Now, now, Huntress, don't underestimate your prey," Ryn chides. "I can talk and show you at the same time."

He grinds into me slowly, the leather of his Narwagh armor rough against my sensitive skin in a way I really like. I lean forward and nip at his bottom lip, and a satisfied purr rumbles in his chest. The sound has me wondering if his gryphon is as horny and unapologetic as mine is. His full lips skim mine, and it focuses my thoughts solely on the feel of him against me. He doesn't move to kiss me or fuck me; he seems content on simply teasing my mouth...my breasts...my pussy.

I growl in protest, and it seems to amuse him even more.

"You think you want the climax right now, but you're a huntress, Falon. You need to stalk it," he tells me, running the tip of his nose up the side of my neck in a very delicious way. "You need to chase," he declares, bringing his lips temptingly close to mine and then pulling back when I try to close the distance. "You need to lust for the kill," he states matter-of-factly as he starts to grind rhythmically between my thighs.

I moan and tilt my hips in a way that increases the friction between us.

Ryn kisses me finally, drinking down the moans his body is coaxing from me. His tongue twirls with mine, his lips suck at mine and nip. He kisses me so thoroughly that I almost come from that alone. Ryn reads my body like it's his favorite book, and he pulls back just as I get close to riding my release over the edge. I whimper, putty in his capable hands, and he chuckles.

"See, Falon, you have everything you need right here. Treno isn't going to hunt or be hunted. He isn't going to break you open one thrust at a time like you need. He doesn't know you well enough to know when you need to dominate or be dominated."

"Ryn," I snarl. "Shut the fuck up about Treno and get inside of me!"

Ryn's eyes light up with victory, and he rolls off of me onto his back. I don't need an invitation, and I climb on top of him, grabbing the neck of his gouged armor vest and pulling him until he's sitting. Fire is banked in his gaze, and I can feel his eyes on me like they're his hands as he looks from my lips to my breasts. I untie the vest and pull it off. I shove the tunic underneath roughly over his head and then move down lower.

I untie the laces over his hips and cock, skimming the dark brown curls that peek out of the top of his pants. I can see the outline of him pressing against the animal skin of his pants, and I can't help but lick my lips. I want my mouth around him. I need to taste his want and feel his needy fingers in my hair as I swallow him down.

Ryn tilts his hips up as I get his pants untied, and I pull them off his well-muscled thighs, down his calves and...shit. I forgot about his boots. I quickly yank them off, one foot at a time, and by the time I get Ryn fully naked, I'm so wet and ready that I'm pretty sure I'm going to come before he can even get inside of me. He watches me just as hungrily, and I crawl back up his legs and palm him. He's shiny with desire, and I stick my tongue out, eager to taste how his lust is flavored. His hips jerk up, and he hisses as I run my tongue up the underside of his cock.

My hard nipples skim his thighs as I wrap my lips around his head. I bob shallowly at first and then gradually take Ryn deeper and deeper into my throat. I hum appreciatively when he moans my name. Wrapping my palm around his base, I work in time with my mouth to make him feel like I'm taking all of him in my throat.

I clench around nothing as he threads his fingers in my hair, bucking into my mouth and worshipping me with his moans and praise. Out of nowhere, he pulls my mouth off his cock and pulls my lips up to his.

"Hey!" I protest, and he laughs.

"I want to come in your cunt, Falon, not your throat," he declares, his lips kissing me into submission.

He pulls away and palms my breast, dropping his mouth to suck on my nipples as I reach down and position him at my entrance. I drop down on top of him, and sure enough, I come right away. Incredible sensation shoots out to the tips of my body and then gets sucked back to where his cock is buried deep inside of me. I ride him and my orgasm as it ricochets through my body.

I grind against his base until his brown curls are soaked with my release and his lips are against my ear.

"Yes, that's where you belong, my Huntress. Your body against mine, your lips screaming my name, your cum all over my dick, my mouth, my fingers. This is where you should always be, and this is my place now too. I live now to feel you spasm with pleasure around me. I exist to worship you, your mind, your heart, your body. You're mine now," Ryn declares.

He flips me onto my back and lets his body claim me the way his words are trying to. I throw my head back and float on all the exquisite sensations his dick and mouth are calling from my body. He nips at my neck and jaw, palms my breasts, and he fucks me hard. It's all so good that my staccato moans turn into a steady thrum of just his name spilling out of my lips. Ryn bites at my shoulder hard enough to register the pressure but not enough to break the skin. He buries himself between my thighs and roars out his release, the meat of my shoulder still between his teeth. His thrusts get more and more shallow as he empties himself inside of me. Then suddenly, just when it seems like things are slowing down, he grinds into me, and it hits everything just right and sends me over the edge one more time.

He plays with my nipples as I come apart again, chuckling when I slap his hands away. He rests his forehead between my breasts, and we both work to catch our breaths. He doesn't pull out of me, and for some reason, I'm grateful for that. It's as though we're floating in this in-between world of pleasure and connection and intimacy. But the minute he moves, it will shatter. I'll have to crash back down to a world where I don't belong, dealing with shit that's way out of my paygrade.

I just want to stay in this moment, Ryn between my thighs, pleasure echoing in ripples of warmth through me.

I play with the short strands of his brown hair. The light catches streaks of blond as the locks move through my fingers, and it's like the sun is proudly pointing out all the places it's kissed his soft hair over time. Ryn's fingers trace up and then back down my sides in a slow, hypnotizing rhythm.

"We'll be leaving by the end of the week," he tells me, his voice and body relaxed against mine.

"What?" I ask, surprised by that statement.

He looks up at me, his gray eyes studying my face. "I had to change the normal exit strategy to accommodate you and several others who have been working behind the scenes here, but it's all arranged. Five more days, and we can all be free of this place forever."

"And go where?" I ask.

Ryn's brow dips as if he thinks the question is odd. "We go with the Hidden and put an end to this war once and for all," he states, like it should be obvious.

Zeph's face surfaces slowly in my mind until it comes into focus. It's as though I can still feel his hands around my throat and see the way his face contorted with cold rage when he told me to leave. His words play back in my head as if he's snarling them at me still.

"Get home if you can, hide if you can't, and hope a Cynas gets to you before the Avowed can, or worse, the Ouphe dregs track you down."

"You'll throw me to the wolves, just like that?"

"It's where your kind belongs. Oh and, Falon, if you ever come back here, I'll kill you myself."

Ryn's fingers tracing up my side pull me from the memory, and I shiver, not able to help it. Ryn doesn't notice, seemingly lost in his own thoughts. I watch as he debates something for a moment. His eyes go far away for a beat and then they focus on me again as he settles on a decision.

"I was sent here to find information on what Zeph and I think might be a secret weapon. I found it, and now we can destroy the Vow once and for all," he tells me, like this solves everything.

"Wow," I state in response, not sure what else to say.

Ryn must hear hesitation in my tone, because he sits back, like my lack of excitement just slapped him across the face. He pulls out of me, and just like I suspected, I feel the peace around us shatter. I sit up, and we both stare at each other for a moment.

"What am I missing here?" he finally asks, and I release a deep weary breath.

"I can't go back, Ryn. I want you to be where you're safe, so I understand that you have to go, but that's not an option for me. I'm still trying to get home, and I think I may be able to figure out how...here."

The line in my mother's journal about my gran finding a way for them to be safe resonates in my mind. Gran was a gryphon, and yet she must have figured out that there was something going on with the gates. I'm hoping there's a book or something in the archives that will help me figure them out. It may take ages to find it, but I sure as hell won't find it with the Hidden. Especially not if Zeph kills me, like he promised to do.

Ryn's eyes harden, and his nostrils flare with anger. I can tell he's trying to control his breathing, but the fury is etched all over his face.

"Your place is here, Falon. This is home now," he declares, slapping his palm against his chest. He angrily gestures in the direction of Kestrel City. "You can't stay here. It's not safe, and I can't just leave you. That's not in me."

"Ryn..." I start. "Zeph—"

"This isn't about Zeph!" Ryn snaps, cutting me off. "I

know you two got off on the wrong foot, but he doesn't trust easily. If you knew what he has been through—"

"I don't fucking care what he's been through," I shout at Ryn, not meaning it, but pissed all the same.

I get up and move in the direction of my clothes. Ryn steps in my way.

"He put his hands around my throat and told me if he ever saw me again, he'd kill me. This *is* about Zeph, and I *can't* go back."

Ryn opens his mouth to argue, but I shut it down.

"We fucked, it's fine. You don't owe me anything, and I don't expect anything. I'm not some weepy girl who gets too attached because you stuck your dick in me. Maybe I'm not safe here, but I wasn't safe with the Hidden either. I wish you all the best with this war. I just hope I can get as far away from it as possible," I tell him, and then I try to step around him.

He blocks my path again.

"Falon, you are coming with me. That's the end of it. You can trust me to protect you."

Ryn's words and tone are harsh. They lash out at me like a whip that not only wants to sting me with each crack but bind me so I can't escape. Pigeon rustles uneasily inside of me as if she's uncomfortable watching her friends fight and doesn't know what to do about it.

I huff out a resigned breath, and my eyes soften. I step into Ryn like a good little gryphon that's submitting. He relaxes slightly and brings his hands up to rub my shoulders comfortingly. Before he can touch me, I bring my knee up hard against his unprotected and uncovered balls.

Ryn gasps and folds in on himself. I waste no time sprinting away and leaping up toward the dipping sun. Pigeon takes over, shifting us right on cue, and we race back toward Kestrel City. I don't look back at Ryn; I know he'll recover soon and we don't have a second to waste. If I can stay near the Avowed, he'll stay away from me. He can't afford for his cover to be blown over some misguided sense of responsibility. We'll both be better off if we just go our separate ways and forget anything ever happened between us.

13

A booming knock on my door echoes around the room, and I glare at it as I towel dry my hair. I feel like shit, I had a horrible dream where I was burning alive, and then I woke up and had the weirdest fucking hot flashes. I think I slept maybe three hours, and I got up feeling achy and gross.

I just finished a long bath and was debating crawling back into bed for the rest of the day.

The only problem with that plan is that I'm not sure if Ryn can kidnap me from here. I haven't seen him since our altercation yesterday, but I'm not stupid enough to think the arrogant prick won't try something.

The knock sounds off again.

"Flower? Are you there?" Treno asks on the other side of the door, and relief and excitement start pumping through me.

"Calm down, bro! You just got your itch scratched yesterday, and look how well that turned out for us," I point out to Pigeon as she gets all fangirly inside of me.

I open the door and look up to find Treno's smiling face. Damn. I forgot how tall he was.

"Did I wake you?" he asks, looking over my head at the crumpled bedding that's askew all over the bed.

"No, come in," I offer, stepping out of the way and opening the door wider. "How are you?" I ask a little awkwardly.

I haven't seen him in a while, and it's like someone hit the reset button on my feeling easy and comfortable around him, and now we're just stiff and awkward. He walks in and looks around. I run through a short list of small talk options, but they all revolve around what he's been up to these days and what's new. I already know he was off doing war shit, but I feel wrong asking about that. Like somehow I'm betraying Treno, Zeph, and Ryn by inserting myself in the middle just by asking questions or being told about it.

I'm trying hard to be motherfucking Switzerland in this Avowed, Hidden showdown. Well, maybe not Switzerland exactly, as I think what the Avowed did—and are doing—is pretty fucked up. But either way, I doubt I'll be helping anyone by shoving my nose in any of it.

"I want to apologize again for leaving the way I did. I wish there had been some other way, but my hands were tied. I swear to you, if it hadn't been life or death, I would have never left you after—"

"It's fine really," I offer hastily.

He looks so upset, and I feel bad. I hope he doesn't think I'm mad at him. His notes pop up in my mind and worry trickles through me. Shit. Was I supposed to write him back? I didn't even think of that. No wonder he's all grovel-y.

"I got your notes," I reassure him. "I completely understand."

"You do?" he asks, surprised.

"Of course! You have a duty to your people; I would never take offense to you putting that over me. I've been fine," I tell him.

I offer a smile, and he studies me for a beat and then visibly relaxes. "I was so worried," he admits, and I chuckle and reach out to rub his bicep comfortingly.

Damn, it's like petting a boulder.

Heat stirs in me, and I flip off Pigeon in my head.

"I can't tell you how relieved I am to hear that we're okay," he tells me, pulling me in for a tight hug.

I wrap my arms around his torso, unable to stop myself from soaking up the warm affection. It seems I'm like a moth to flame these days when it comes to people being nice to me.

"I know I just got back, but I made plans to make my absence up to you. I have the whole day planned, and I vow there will be no disappearing or leaving anything unfinished," he tells me, stepping back so he can look at my face. His eyes are earnest, and his offer is adorable.

I hesitate for a second, eyeing my bed and wondering if he'll take a raincheck. His face falls ever so slightly, and something in my stomach does too.

"If...if you don't want to, I, of course, understand," he states, and even his chin dimple looks bummed.

"No, it's not that at all. I'd love to spend the day with you. I just need to grab something to eat first. I skipped breakfast, and I have a little bit of a headache," I explain, the thought of yummy food now all I can focus on.

"Then to the kitchens we go," he announces, offering his arm. I take it and chuckle as he leads me out of my room. His excitement and eagerness is contagious. I forgot how good I always feel around him, which is weird because we haven't spent *that* much time together. I shrug and go with it. It's a nice change from all the broody shit I've been dealing with since I got here.

* * *

Treno lays down a blanket, and I look around and wipe at some of the sweat gathering on the back of my neck. It's supposed to be the cold season sneaking in to displace the warmth, but it feels like the warm season decided it wasn't going to go quietly. Suddenly the barely there dresses popular in Kestrel City make a shit ton more sense. For the first time since I was forced into one, I wish I had gone with the scantily clad dress instead of the Narwagh hide pants, bra, and vest.

Treno sits on the blanket and starts unpacking the picnic basket he had prepared for us this morning while I was stuffing my face. He tugs at his own braided armor vest, and I feel better knowing I'm not the only one turning into some kind of sweat beast here.

He looks up at me and gives me a shy smile that cracks me up. He's been so nervous today as we've puttered around Kestrel City and checked out what there is to check out. This gorgeous, ripped, Altern of the Avowed is nervous around *me* for some reason, and it's proving to be seriously entertaining. I mean, I practically unhinged my jaw and consumed a whole slab of meat this morning in an effort to satiate my ravenous appetite, and yet he's been looking at me all day like I'm some kind of prize.

I snort and Pigeon wing fives me in my head. She gets it. It makes no fucking sense that he's even looking my way, but you won't hear me complaining. I sit down on the blanket and scoot over until I'm in the shade. Treno's mismatched gaze fills with satisfaction, and I wonder if he only put half the blanket in the shade on purpose so I'd end up sitting closer to him.

"So, flower, I'd like to sit here and eat all kinds of sweet things and hear all about you," he announces, grabbing a piece of dark purple fruit that's the color of a plum but shaped like a strawberry on steroids.

He takes a bite of the fruit and leans back on his elbows, watching me the whole time. I chuckle.

"Um, okay, what exactly do you want to know?" I ask, not sure where to even start when it comes to me. Between the journal I read days ago and the memories that surface more and more every day, I'm not even sure what the CliffsNotes version of *me* should contain anymore.

"I want to know whatever you want to tell me," he states wisely, showing interest but keeping the ball in my court.

It's been ages since I've been out on a proper date. Mostly because, as a latent, shifters took issue with me, and I'd never found a Non I was interested in. But as odd as the timing of today is, it's been nice spending time with Treno. I like getting to know him, and it makes me look at the conflict between the Hidden and the Avowed differently. There's a human element to both sides now, and it soothes something in me that I can't quite explain.

"Well...I'm twenty-five. I am a mechanic, or at least I used to be, where I come from."

"What's a mechanic?" he asks, reaching across me to grab some overgrown edamame-looking thingy.

"That's a hard one, because you have no idea what cars or automobiles are, and that's what I used to fix, but the short answer is I fix things."

"We're going to circle back to whatever cahhs are, but you fixing things is intriguing. So you're telling me my flower is beautiful, wise and understanding, *and* smart?" he teases. "By the stars, could a being be so blessed?"

I laugh and breathe on my nails, buffing them out on my vest. "What can I say, the gate chose wisely," I tease.

"That it did, that it did," he agrees, his eyes bright and his smile catching.

"So what about you?" I ask, feeling more relaxed in spite of the sweltering heat.

"Ooh, we're on me already?" he asks with a faux nervous look.

I laugh, and he tilts his head to the side in thought.

"Well, I'm the Altern..." he starts, and I snort and give him a look that says *oh really, I had no idea*.

He chuckles.

"What all does that entail?" I ask, repeating the pattern of him asking about what I did.

"Mostly, it's me doing everything my brother isn't interested in...which is pretty much everything not involving the war. He's very focused on victory and not much else, which means the rest falls on me. A lot of boring planning for crops and maintaining the city and its defenses."

"Mogus extermination," I add cheekily.

"Naturally," he replies not missing a beat, his smile stretching even wider.

"Do you like being the second in command?" I press, picking up on an undercurrent of melancholy in his tone.

He looks at me for a beat like he's trying to see into my head while also trying to sort out what's in his own.

"Would you think I'm addled if I told you no?" he asks, the smile on his face never wavering, but I don't miss the glint of insecurity in his mismatched gaze.

"No way," I reassure him. "I wouldn't want the job if it were offered to me," I add.

"And your reasoning for that would be..." he queries, trailing off.

"That's a lot of pressure. Yes, there are perks, I'm sure. But to be responsible for all of those people, to have their safety, livelihood, prosperity, and happiness sitting on my shoulders..." I trail off, and Treno nods, his look far away.

"Maybe I'd feel different if it weren't for the war, but the battles get tiring. We make progress, then lose ground... It's a never-ending, stagnant trap. Lazza won't hear anything against it; if you're not there to discuss strategy, then he has no time for you. I wondered often what he'd be like once it's all over, but I can't picture it anymore," he states evenly, his tone somewhat sad.

I watch Treno for a beat as he gets lost in some unspoken thought. He looks so sad and resigned in this moment, and I'm surprised by how impacted I feel by that. I can't imagine what he's been through, and it's clear the fighting has taken its toll. I want to soothe the ache I hear in his voice and chase away the shadows in his eyes.

"So, if you weren't the Altern, what would you be doing right now?" I ask, changing the direction of the conversation from gloomy to lighter hypotheticals.

"Wow," Treno states, his eyes thoughtful. "I'm not sure." He laughs and shakes his head. "One of my best friends growing up wanted to be a farmer. At the time, I thought that it seemed like too much work, but now..." He pauses. "Now, I think I'd really like that life—maybe not crops, but animals. I've always liked working with creatures. Just the thought of working hard, coming home to my mate and my eyas, living off of my own efforts and abilities...yeah, that sounds like a good life to me."

Treno gives me a warm smile that I feel settle deep in my chest.

"Now tell me all about cahhs," he requests, and I crack up.

"You sound like you're from Boston the way you say that," I point out, grabbing the lovechild between a plum and an Arnold Schwarzenegger sized strawberry and taking a bite.

Juice drips down the side of my mouth, and I'm forced to give the loudest, most unladylike slurp known to man to keep this fruit from jizzing all over me. Treno laughs and wipes at my cheeks with his hands in an effort to stop the greatest juice tsunami of our time. There's no hope, and sticky sweetness drips down my vest to mix with the sweat and make things even more uncomfortable for me.

I pull the fruit away from my mouth and announce, "She's a squirter!"

I pause for a minute as what I just said sinks in, and then I completely lose it. I start laughing so hard I must look like a braying donkey. Treno clearly has no idea what I find so funny, but apparently my gleeful giggles are contagious, because he's guffawing in no time right alongside me.

"You made it look so sexy," I accuse as we dive right into another set of giggle fits. "You could have warned me about the level of juiciness I was up against!"

"And miss this? So long as we both live, you can count on me to *never* warn you about possible food mishaps! This was just too good. Who knew sak fruit could be this entertaining?"

"It's called sak fruit?" I demand, new peals of laughter ringing out of me. "That makes it so much worse!"

"It does, doesn't it," he agrees on a chuckle.

The next thing I know, Treno has a hold of my hips, and he's pulling me closer to him. Before I can even squeak in surprise, his lips are on mine. I'm a little stunned by the sudden move but not mad at it in the least. He cups my now sticky cheeks and moves his lips from my top lip to my bottom and back up again. I lean into him and open up, ready to see just where he wants to take this.

He promptly takes it to the ninth ring of *holy motherfucking shit, this guy just kissed me right into an orgasm*. Then he brings me back down to spend a little time in *can you get pregnant from kissing, because I think I just did* land. And then finally we end up in a solid state of *I'm going to go ahead and need you to fuck me now*.

Treno pulls back, and with not an ounce of shame, I lean

forward to chase his lips. He runs his thumb over my now kiss-swollen mouth, and if I were wearing panties, they would have spontaneously combusted by now.

Consider my world...rocked.

"Holy shit," I mumble at the same time Treno breathes, "Wow." I know that mouth-fuck was all him, but I won't argue with any appreciation he wants to throw my way.

"I'm sorry," he tells me, his mismatched eyes studying mine. "You were laughing, and I wanted to taste the pure joy as it poured out of your mouth. I have to say, it's better than the sak fruit," he teases, and I giggle like an oversexed schoolgirl.

Pigeon gives me the side-eye and I'm pretty sure flashes me some version of *don't mess this up for us, you weirdo!*

I shove her away.

"Never apologize for doing *that*...ever again," I inform him, and he laughs.

"Good to know," he confesses, and then he closes the distance between us again.

I'm so ready to get lost in another epic kiss. There's just one fucking problem. It's hot as hell, and I'm suddenly sticky and itchy where the fruit juice went down my top. How is a girl supposed to ride a man's face into happy oblivion with this sticky, sweaty, itchy situation going on? I'm pretty sure if I just ripped all of my clothes off right now, Treno would take that as a good thing. That might help with the sweaty, but the sticky and itchy are still going to be a problem. Maybe I can convince him to go back to the city where I can ride his face in the shower?

"Where'd you go?" he asks me, sucking on my bottom lip and then nipping at it in a way that coaxes out a moan.

"You are so fucking hot, but so am I. I'm dying," I tell him, pulling at the collar of my top.

"Oh, thank the Thais Fairies, I thought it was just me," he confesses. "Do you care if I take my armor off? I didn't want to be presumptuous, but I think the liquid currently trapped in my armor could rival that of a sak fruit's."

I laugh and gesture for him to go ahead.

"Can I take mine off too?" I ask, the need to itch overwhelming any decency or sexiness I might have been hoping to accomplish.

"Of course! Are you okay?" he queries, as I immediately shove my hand down the V of the vest and scratch aggressively between my breasts.

"I'm super fucking itchy all of a sudden," I admit, and he nods his head like this information isn't at all surprising.

"Let's go for a swim. It will wash off the juice, which should cure the itching and cool us both down." He gestures over at a small lake to our right, and as much as unfamiliar water freaks me out, I could orgasm alone at the thought of swimming in crisp cool water.

"Last one to the water has to sweat more," I declare lamely, but it's too fucking hot to be witty.

I sprint toward the lake, untying my clothes as I go. Treno yells an objection and then laughs as he rushes to catch up with me. I rip my top off and practically attack the evil bra underneath. Why the fuck do I even bother wearing these? I shred the laces with a well-placed talon and fling it away from me. I almost eat dirt while trying to get my pants off, but yesterday's mistakes are today's triumphs. I recover and *hoot* in victory, naked and feeling infinitely better already.

Strong arms grab me from behind, and the next thing I know, I'm lifted up and thrown caveman style over Treno's shoulder. We reach the edge of the lake in a couple of his long strides when he grabs me off his shoulder, and I can tell he's going to throw me in. I squeal my protest, and it comes out like the bleat of a constipated goat. I hold onto his arms for dear life and scream *noooooo!*

Maybe it was the creepy goat noise or the blood curdling scream, but Treno stops mid throw and brings me eye level with him instead.

"What happened?" he asks, holding me out in front of him.

I gesture to the water. "There's not anything that lives in there that's going to, like, eat me?" I ask, eyeing the lake now like it just might be poison. "Anything that's going to try to crawl into an orifice and lay eggs?" I add, feeling like that's a good one to ask about too.

Treno looks at me like I'm crazy.

Pshhh, swallowing down my breakfast whole and angry itching my boobs, he doesn't bat a lash at, but asking about possible scary lake predators gets me the judgy eyes?

Treno cracks up and starts shaking his head. "No, nothing that's going to gobble you up except for me," he states casually. And then the fucker throws me unceremoniously into the lake while I scream, "What about the egg thing?"

I pull in a deep breath mid-flight and hit the water with an epic cannonball worthy splash. I sink into the cool water, and it feels so good he's immediately forgiven for the throwing. It's surprisingly clear, and I instantly feel better that if there is anything that might want to lay eggs in my anus, I'll see it coming.

A massive male form drops into the water on my left, and I kick up to the surface with a gasp and smooth strands of hair back from my face. Treno pops up laughing, and I immediately rain my wrath in the form of splashes down upon him. He quickly retaliates, showing no mercy whatsoever, and that's when I pull out the big guns.

Wings shove out of my back, and I immediately recruit them to aid in my assault. Treno may have me beat on the splashing front because his arms are so fucking long and big, but so is my wingspan. Treno calls on his own wings, but I'm hammering him with so much water he's going to need to start calling me Niagara Falls. He shouts and huddles over, lifting one white wing and waving it like a flag of surrender.

I pause my watery onslaught. "Do you give up?" I ask, victory and amusement sprinkled through my tone.

He turns to me, a wry smile on his face. "Never!" he declares and leaps for me. I squeal and try to splash him into submission again, but he's too fast.

"Cheater!" I scream-giggle as I turn and try to escape the arms winding around me like octopus tentacles.

"How dare you!" Treno mock gasps. "The mistake of trusting me was yours, flower," he teases, and I wiggle, weak with laughter, to get out of his hold.

I'm about as effective as a floundering fish out of water, but I can't stop laughing.

Treno turns me until we're chest to chest, and his smile and answering laughter make me feel all warm and gooey inside.

"First rule of battle, flower. Never give your opponent the benefit of the doubt. They'll use it against you every time," he jokes as he pins me tightly against him.

My purple gaze grows devilish, and I shove my hand between our slippery bodies to grab his cock. I circle my hand around it and smile when he freezes.

"Second rule of battle, Treno," I parrot cheekily. "Never leave your cock unprotected, it'll get used against you every time," I tell him saucily, leaning in until our lips are a mere hair's breadth away.

"You've caught me with my wings bound and my pants

down," he admits on a breathy chuckle, his hard-on jerking slightly in my grasp. "Then again, I could say the same thing," he adds, dropping his hand from my waist and running his fingers through the folds of my pussy.

Want fills his blue and purple gaze, and I nip at his bottom lip.

"Mmmmm. What can I say, you got me," I admit, my voice dripping with need. I lean back, spreading my legs and giving him better access.

His other hand drops slightly to support me better in the water, and I internally cheer. Just as Treno licks his lips and moves his fingertips to circle my clit, I use my wings and arms to start splashing him again. He yelps in surprise, releasing me, and I hurry back and give myself a better position for victory.

Treno laughs and shields himself again.

"First rule of battle!" I shout out, smug as fuck.

"Truce...Truce!" Treno calls out, and I stop my attack and pull my wings into my back.

He swims slowly toward me as I tread water and hungrily watch his languid approach.

"Beautiful, wise and understanding, smart, and...diabolical," he tells me, adding to the list of my qualities that he named earlier.

"And never forget it," I tease, booping his nose when he's close enough.

He reaches out and pulls me to him again. I wrap my legs around his waist and take in the feel of his large hard body against mine. I don't know what I'm going to do without these giant sized males and all their giant sized parts if I ever get home. It's very possible that I might be ruined.

He has several tattoos on his arms, and I find myself

wanting to trace them with my fingers and then with my tongue. He has a large symbol on the inside of both his biceps and a horizontal line of smaller symbols over his left pec. Something about them feels familiar, and I get the distinct impression I've seen them before.

"Ahh, that's better," Treno observes as he fits us together

A flash of Ryn fucking me yesterday and telling me that I belong with him, just like that...forever, pops up in my mind, shattering the odd sensation I have about Treno's tattoos. I shove everything away and focus on the here and now. "It is," I agree breathily, and Pigeon shoves her enthusiastic *I'm also on board* through me, and I chuckle.

Treno's eyes ask me what's so funny.

"My gryphon has plenty of favorable opinions and ideas about what she'd like us to be doing right now," I tell him on a laugh.

For a split second, worry ripples through me, and I wonder if Treno will think my relationship with Pigeon is strange. Sutton's voice, telling me that I have to be one with my gryphon, fills my head. I fret that even though Treno's connection with his gryphon seems more like mine, what if I'm wrong and he doesn't understand?

His answering laugh breaks through my anxiety.

"You'd be scandalized if I told you the things mine has been wanting to do since he first saw her," he tells me, talking about his connection as if it's just like mine. "We'll have to give them plenty of time to *solidify their bonds* just as soon as..."

Treno trails off, and his lips claim mine. He swallows my chuckle at the gentle use of *solidify their bonds* instead of saying what we're both thinking, which is *gryphon fuck their brains out*. My tongue tangles with his, and it hits me that I've never really thought about Pigeon fucking other gryphons. I mean, she's shown me enough imagery that really her desire to do just that shouldn't be a shock, but I guess I'm learning slowly how to be an *us* instead of just a *me*.

"What are you thinking about?" Treno asks me against my lips.

"That I can be selfish," I answer bluntly, and he chuckles and pulls back.

"Who isn't?" he asks, like it's that simple.

I shrug and lean in to resume that thing he was just doing with his tongue.

He pulls back, denying me his lips, and I squeak out a noise of protest.

"Every time I start to play with you, you get distracted," he tells me, his tone light but his words serious. "If you keep doing that, I'm going to develop a complex," he razzes.

"Fuck, I'm sorry. I don't know what my deal is; I'm not normally this scatterbrained," I confess.

I run my fingers through his white wet locks and grind against him lightly.

"I'll stop being annoying. My body is ready," I announce with a cheeky smile.

Treno returns it, but he still hesitates.

"We don't have to...if you're not feeling it," he offers, his blue and purple eyes studying mine.

Pigeon shoves her irritation at me, and I side-eye her.

"Alright, already," I defend. *"If you'd stop interrupting, I could focus!"* I accuse.

"It's not that," I reassure him. "I do want you, and I am ready...so fucking ready...I promise."

I open my mouth to explain that I just have a lot on my mind and that a lot has happened in the past couple of days, but I shut up instead. That shit sounds lame even to me. I have a hot as fuck, body of a god, dimple-chinned male between my thighs, and I don't know what my fucking problem is.

Get your fucking head in the fuck game, Falon!

14

I release a deep breath and run my thumb over his cheek. I don't say another word. I lean in and capture his lips with mine. I focus on the feel of his mouth and tongue. I hone in on his hands as one buries itself at my nape and the other drops low on my back, pinning me tightly against him. I revel in the feel of his hard abs between my thighs—I could probably ride those alone into an epic orgasm.

Treno responds to my newfound focus with appreciative groans and encouraging thrusts of his hips against mine. He walks us up and out of the water, kissing me thoroughly as he takes us back to the picnic blanket. I go full koala, happy to let him do all the legwork. My inner cavewoman is a massive fan of the *big strong man* skills he's displaying, and I practically swoon when he lays me back on the blanket like the delicate flower he thinks I am.

I expect him to move slowly up my naked body, to kiss me sensually and memorize my body with his worship-filled hands. But I get a delicious lesson in how wrong I am in thinking Treno could ever be a predictable softy. He buries his face between my thighs like a ravenous beast, and

I scream out my surprise and then moan my approval when he sucks on my clit and looks up at me like he's the devil himself and I have no idea what I just got myself into.

I thread my fingers through his hair and watch him lick me up and down, sucking on my lips and clit, and fucking me with his tongue. It's so fucking erotic, and even if I couldn't feel him all over my pussy, I could probably come just from watching what he's doing. He plays my body with his mouth like he was born for it, and I splinter into pure pleasure that has me grinding against his face in no time.

If I thought he'd go gentle now that I've just come all over his mouth, I'd once again be wrong, because Treno is acting like now that he has my attention, he's never going to let it go. I mewl and writhe as he pins my hips and devours me. He grunts and groans as I fight him, and he easily puts me right back in my place. I'm stuck in this weird place where I'm too sensitive and also need more.

Please do the vibrating tongue thing. Please do the vibrating tongue thing.

Pigeon high fives my brilliance, and we both watch eagerly as Treno looks up, his tongue extended and pressed against my clit...and then he does the motherfucking vibrating tongue thing. I explode into nothing and everything all at once. I scream his name and feel my body break apart on a wave of ecstasy. Pigeon cheers inside of me, and it's so loud I feel like my body is a stadium housing some kind of sporting event.

He vibrates me into another orgasm, and then he takes mercy on me. Moving up my body, he languidly kisses the ticklish spots around my hip bones and abdomen. He cups my breasts and then forces me to lose my mind again when he does the vibrating tongue thing to my nipples. I moan and whimper and scream my approval, and then I kiss the fuck out of him when his lips are within attacking distance.

I can taste my desire on his tongue, but I'm not even fussed about it. It's not going to earn so much as a nose wrinkle from me, because anyone who can do what he just did deserves to be worshipped, and I am up for the task. I roll my hips against him, my pussy begging to take his cock for a ride. I wrap my hand around him and start working him slowly root to tip, while I break up our kiss and move my mouth to his ear.

"You feel so fucking good," I purr, stroking him leisurely, his wetness coating my palm and smoothing out my rhythm. "You want to fuck me, Treno? You want to shove this cock deep in my pussy while I scream your name?" I ask him, and he groans deeply in reply and sucks at my neck.

He drops a hand between us and pushes fingers inside of me, and I purr and grind against the palm of his hand.

"You make me so fucking wet. Do you feel how much I want you? I want you so deep inside of me, fucking me hard and fast. Do you want to fuck me?" I ask.

This time, Treno nips at my earlobe and growls a resounding *yes*. "I need to be inside of you, flower. I need to claim you. I need to feel you clench around me as I fill you up and make you mine," he rumbles in my ear, and even more desire flutters through my limbs at his words and needy tone.

"Then fuck me," I command.

Treno snarls his approval, biting down on my earlobe, and lines himself up with me. I'm so fucking wet that his size isn't even an issue as he buries his cock balls deep between my thighs.

"Yes," I shout over and over again, my praise and encouragement punctuating each deep perfectly timed thrust.

I pull my knees back, opening myself up as wide as I can to accommodate his large body. We both shout out at the new deeper connection, and he takes over, pressing down on my knees, spreading me and using the hold as leverage. I shove my fingers in his hair and pull lightly so there's just a hint of delicious pressure at his roots, and Treno's sensual growl lets me know he loves it. He leans in and sucks on my bottom lip as he rolls his hips with each thrust. He gets so fucking deep it feels like he's lighting up every nerve ending I have between my thighs.

"Fuck yes! Make me come, just like that...make me fucking come!" I order, and he leans down his mouth to my ear, clearly taking a page out of my book.

"You like that, flower? Like when I own you and work you into a frenzy? Mmmm, you feel so good around my cock. Come all over it like you did my tongue. Scream my name and come for me, flower."

Treno whispers all the best dirty shit in my ear, and I could practically cry from the massive orgasm I feel building in my cells.

"Harder," I bark out. "Yes, right there! Fuck, I'm going to come...right there..."

I scream and shatter as Treno fucks me into the best fucking orgasm ever. He comes inside of me, kissing me and mumbling incoherent shit like *mate* and *mine* against my lips. I'm so fucking exhausted as release tingles through me like waves, and all I want to do is sleep and then wake up and fuck him all over again. I want to spend weeks on this dude's dick, and even then, it might not be enough.

Fuck, that was good!

Treno chuckles and rolls onto his back, panting. He laces his fingers with mine and brings my hand up to his mouth and kisses it sweetly. Pigeon is giving him a standing ovation, and I get the distinct impression that she flings a *my turn* at me. And that throws me off.

"You can't fuck Treno; that's weird, you creep."

Pigeon rolls her eyes at me and then flashes me Treno's

white gryphon—and a brief synopsis of everything she'd like to do with him. My eyebrows shoot up to my hairline, and I beg her to stop.

"How the fuck is that even possible? You know what...I don't want to know, keep your perv to yourself, okay?"

Pigeon chuckles and flashes me an image of an Amish woman.

"Did you just call me a prude?" I demand, completely offended. *"First of all, rude. Second of all, you just watched what Treno and I did together, so you know that's bullshit."*

Smug satisfaction flickers through me, and I can tell that somehow Pigeon thinks I'm making her point. She flashes me another *my turn* and then a memory of me at the movies. I stare at it for a second until I realize what she's trying to say.

"It's my turn to watch?" I ask, trying to confirm that I'm understanding her correctly.

Images of lights and alarms sound off in my head like I just won money in Vegas. I open my mouth to tell her she's lost it when I realize that, if I'm being fair, I may not have much of a choice in this. How can I fuck my brains out but expect her not to?

Treno's laugh pulls me away from the uncomfortable direction of my thoughts.

"You didn't hear any of that, did you?" he asks, rolling to his side and tracing the curve of my breast with his finger.

I offer a sheepish smile.

"What are you thinking about *now*?" he teases good-naturedly.

"Gryphon porn," I reply before I can stop myself.

He barks out a laugh. "Why, by the stars, are you thinking about that?"

"I don't know, it just hit me. How does it work? Do we just hang around and watch like perverts? Does it feel good to us too? How do you keep your gryphon from humping everything?"

I shoot out questions rapid-fire, and with each one I voice, another pops up in my head. Treno laughs hard and then kisses me softly before pulling back. "I don't actually know what it's like. I haven't experienced it yet, but from—"

"Wait. What?" I ask cutting him off. "You've never allowed your gryphon to let his freak flag fly?"

Shock radiates out of my tone, and Treno's brow dips in confusion.

"Of course not," he defends, like I've just accused him of something seriously fucked up. "When a gryphon mates, it's for life. It's different than when we mate in this form," Treno explains, gesturing to my naked body and his. "We can mate in this form for pleasure, and it doesn't create a bond, that is unless it happens after a mate call. But if a gryphon mates in its gryphon form, those gryphons are immediately bonded for life."

"Oh okay, that makes sense," I state.

"So is it usual for a gryphon to be a massive ball of lust until they mate?" I ask, thinking of Pigeon and all the fucking with my hormones she does.

"No, the opposite is true. A gryphon's mating instinct can only be sparked by their true mate. If they don't find them, then that part of them stays dormant."

My eyebrows crinkle as I think that through.

"Wait...but you said that your gryphon wanted to fuck mine?" I remind him, like somehow there must be a loophole.

Treno laughs like he thinks I just told a hilarious joke. He immediately stops when he realizes I'm not laughing too.

"Well, yes, of course my gryphon wants to mate with

yours because she's his mate," he declares, his eyes filling with concern.

I stare at him for a beat, just...blinking.

"What the fuck is going on?" I suddenly demand. I sit up, and Treno mirrors me, worry etched in his features. "What am I missing here? I mean, I didn't think I was fucking dumb, but clearly I am, because how can our gryphons be mates without us..."

I trail off and take in Treno's encouraging look.

"No," I state matter-of-factly and push up onto my feet.

"What do you mean *no*?" Treno asks, his face and tone bewildered.

"I mean, no, we can't be mates," I answer simply.

A flash of hurt streaks through Treno's mismatched gaze, and then incredulity takes over.

"What are you talking about, flower, you just answered my mate call. How can you say—"

"I what!" I yelp as I round on him, cutting him off.

Shock and frustration filter into his eyes. "You answered my mate call," he repeats like I'm simple.

I throw my hands up in exasperation. "What the fuck, Treno, I never agreed to be your mate! You never even asked me! What are you even talking about?" My voice rises higher and higher in pitch as panic takes over.

"It doesn't work like that," he states, irritation clear in his tone. "Our gryphons put out the call. Usually there's a burning sensation that accompanies the partial bond that's being formed. It can be very painful. The stronger the bond, the more it hurts. You passed out from the pain of ours," he explains, and my stomach drops.

I stare at him horrified.

"Are you being serious right now?" he challenges, his eyes taking me in warily like this is all just a bad joke. "But you had that book about Gryphon mating," he mumbles, almost to himself.

"What?" I ask even more confused.

"The book about The Call and Gryphon mating practices. I saw it on your table."

"No," I answer hollowly. "I found that with all of the census records and took it so I could give it to an Archivist."

We both stare at each other blankly.

"I thought you knew. I mentioned you answering the call in my note...you responded to me...your gryphon responded to us..."

Reality sucker punches me like a fucking semi.

Zeph.

Ryn.

This is what they were keeping from me.

I gasp and try to shove the shock and betrayal back down my throat with my hands.

This is why Pigeon was so upset...she knew.

She. Fucking. Knew.

I fold in on myself, and Treno catches me.

I turn to Pigeon, consumed by hurt and betrayal.

"Why?" is all I can ask as everything inside of me shatters.

Our bond fractures and morphs into something painful and wrong. Everything I've been through since I've arrived, the emotions and connections I didn't understand. The feelings inside that betrayed what was really good for me. She knew about all of it and never bothered to tell me anything.

I clutch at my stomach and wish there was a way I could rip her out of me. I feel tainted, destroyed from the inside out, and there's no way I can purge it. Pigeon hammers me with flashes and impressions, but I lock myself away. I reinforce steel around who I am and vow that no one will ever get inside of it again.

Treno holds me, whispering reassuring things, but I'm too numb to care. How the fuck did I not see this? How did I not ask more questions? How could I just assume this world worked like my own?

Rage lights me up from the inside. I'm so fucking angry I don't even know what to do about it. I'm gutted by Pigeon. Seething over Ryn and Zeph. Pissed at myself, and I don't even know where to begin examining how I feel about Treno. He didn't purposely try to deceive me, but here we are in one big giant clusterfuck anyway.

Silent tears drip down my cheeks. I look up at Treno, who looks stricken, and push out of his lap. He hurries to his feet as I rush to get dressed.

"Where are you going?" he asks, reaching for me again, but dropping his hands when I flinch away.

"Just a word of advice from one mate to another," I snark. "Next time, spell it out as plain as day for her, okay? Double check that she knows exactly what she's in for," I snap as I angrily tie up my laces.

"Next time?" he reels back like I've slapped him. "There won't ever be a next time, Falon. We're it for each other," he states, and part of me wishes that were true.

One clusterfuck might be a hell of a lot more manageable than three. But I don't say that. I need to confirm things first before I go dropping those bombs. I need to find Ryn.

I call on my wings, and Treno finally loses his cool.

"Falon, we need to talk about this. Running isn't going to change anything. I can tell you everything you need to know, and there's a lot more that you need to know."

"That's great, but I need to go freak the fuck out in private for a while. So let's meet up later, and you can tell me all the things, and I'll tell you all the things, and we can go from there," I shout over my shoulder, diving from *enraged* right into *calm and crazy* like they're a better fit.

Treno dives for his pants when it's clear that I'm not going to stick around. I spot more tattoos on his back and calves, but I can't think about that right now, I need to get the fuck out of here. Pigeon surges in my chest, but I slam her back down forcefully. I leap into the air and fly as fast as I can back to the city.

Now to track down Ryn.

15

I sit cross-legged in my bed, the black bound book that Treno thought I had read now pressing down on my lap. I, of course, couldn't find Ryn. That fucker is never around when you need him, so I went to find the next best thing I could think of...the book. Purt, thankfully, wasn't there, and I must have been wearing a look that said if you even talk to me, I will rip you apart, because no one even tried to stop me from leaving with this book in my hands.

Since then, I've barricaded myself in my room...literally. The tree trunk table and gnarled tree limb and stone chairs have been pushed against the doors, not that I need them, because no one has tried to get in. I thought maybe Treno would come and insist on discussing all of the information that apparently I still need to know, but he hasn't. I'm not sure if I'm glad or pissed about that, and the uncertainty of it all has me leaning toward a general state of *I want to fuck everyone up.*

I run my fingers over the words of the page I'm on and shake my head. It's all there. The warm feeling you get when you see a mate outside of your gryphon form. Or the burning and pain you get if you come across them as a gryphon. The drive to mate and seal the bond. The whole wing thing is apparently a big sign—only a mate can force a partial shift or call one back.

The memory of my wings responding to Zeph's and the look on his face. Ryn's wings responding to mine. My wings mirroring Treno's...I swipe the memories away with a growl.

Turning the page, I read on. Irrational jealousy is listed, but I never had that. Mates can apparently soothe each other's gryphons and track each other. In some rare cases, it states, mates can feel each other's emotions and even read each other's minds. I wonder if that means Zeph, Ryn and Treno can feel my rage right now and that's why everyone is staying away. Then again, we might not have that level of connection.

I keep reading.

When the call has been answered, both gryphons will hurt or burn while the bond completely forms. Afterward, they'll feel tired or weak for about a day following. The book says that once the gryphons mate in their form, it strengthens everything, and according to this, the only way to sever a complete connection is through death.

I turn through the several pages of information and warnings. Apparently, once a bond has been formed, the gryphons' essence or life force is linked. Meaning, if someone kills one side of the bond, the other side would probably go too. There are cases mentioned where a mate happened to die when the bond was *not* complete, yet it didn't affect both sides. But there are lots of warnings about that too.

I flip through every page there is, but there isn't anything listed about what to do if you're bonded to lying assholes or to another gryphon that hates you. I do find a chapter on multiple mate bonds though. It's extremely rare but apparently not impossible or unheard of. I thought somehow I would feel better after reading that part, but I don't.

There's a section about smell and mate bonds that leaves me very confused. It states my smell is supposed to change when I'm mated. That the change in smell is supposed to announce to the other members of the Pride that I'm taken. It makes sense that Ryn wouldn't care about that, but I can't figure out why Treno didn't.

Maybe I don't smell? I lift my arm up and sniff under my armpit. Nothing offensive or obvious fills my nose. I make a note to ask Treno about it later. I'm going to fit it in right after I tell him I'm mated to the leader of the Hidden and the Commander who also happens to be a Hidden spy. Maybe the smell question will throw him off just enough that he'll forget he wants to kill me.

I huff out a tired sigh. *Falon, you are a fucking idiot.*

I've been so focused on trying to get home or figure out how to fly and just be a gryphon in general that I ignored obvious signs. Yeah, they do the mate thing very differently from what I've grown up understanding about shifters, but I felt when things were off or didn't make sense. I still dismissed them, and now I'm sorry I did. I spent exactly ten minutes earlier wondering if the gate would somehow sever the mate bonds. If I left, could I survive the pain and longing that apparently occurs? But I keep coming back to how I'm here, why I'm here.

I think it's time I stop dismissing this world as some unimportant flicker and start accepting that this is now my life. A warm confirmation blooms in my chest, and I take a deep breath and embrace it. The warm bloom suddenly feels like a hot coal that's pouring lava through my veins. I get half a yelp out before my jaw locks up and I'm all at once certain of what it feels like to go supernova.

There's a weird explosion of pain that moves through

the searing in my body. It settles inside my upper arms, on my chest, down my back, and at the back of my calves. I grit my teeth and try to ride it out, but something about it tugs at my mind. I know this.

I've felt it before.

That thought cracks something open inside of me, and I shove back in time in my mind.

It's like I'm walking through a living movie, and I can see myself when I was four, maybe, lying in my bed and writhing. I cover my mouth with a shocked hand and watch as black symbols rise up on my skin like they're simply floating to the surface.

Armbands of little symbols ring my forearms in three places. Another four more bands of bigger symbols circle my upper arms. Little me tears at her pajamas, and I can see black marks appearing on the right side of my back like someone is writing a book in an unknown language, and it's all appearing from my shoulder blade down.

My parents run in, and my little body is blocked. My dad is staring at the symbols on my arm with a stunned look on his face. My mom is screaming at him, but I can't make out the details of what they're saying. It's like I'm underwater and wearing ear plugs. My mom wipes hair from my forehead and kisses me. She climbs on the bed and pulls me into her lap. She yells something at my dad, and then I think she starts singing my favorite song. My gran appears at the door. She rushes in and smooths back more sweaty strands of hair that are sticking to my face. She leans into me and tells me things as my mom rocks me in her lap. I watch as little me settles slightly in their arms.

My mom is crying, and my dad is pointing at her and me like he's giving instructions of some sort. My mom suddenly holds me tighter, but not in a soothing way; she's holding me down...she's trying to hold me still. My dad systematically places his hands over the marks that have appeared on my body, and he looks like he's chanting something. *I gasp when I see that one by one the marks are disappearing.*

Little me is screaming. My gran is trying to calm me as my mom holds me tightly, and my dad magically rips the marks from my body.

I pant as I come to, back in the tree room. I don't feel like I passed out, just time traveled through hell. I'm crying. I stare down at my arms. I should have marks there, but I don't. What were they? How did he take them away?

Puzzle pieces fit together in my mind. The Avowed mark pops up in my head, and then the marks on Treno that I stupidly thought were tattoos. The doors that led into the dead Ouphe city of Vedan had similar symbols all over them. They glowed green when the ghost Ouphe Nadi touched them and told them to open.

I didn't see any markings on Zeph or Ryn, not that I've explored every inch of them, but I suspect this is an Ouphe thing. I wonder if everyone who is Ouphe tainted or blessed carries marks of some sort.

I shakily move off the bed and make my way to the bathroom. I strip out of my clothes, and sure enough I have symbols in all the exact places that Treno does. I guess this might just qualify as the "there's so much more you need to know." I make a mental note to never interrupt Treno again. It seems he has important shit to tell me, and I keep cutting him off so he can't.

I feel weak and achy and way fucking worse than I felt after sealing the mate bond with Zeph and Ryn. I draw a bath and clean the residue of sweat and pain from my skin. My new markings aren't sore and don't burn when I expose them to the hot water. They're just...there. For a moment, I'm tempted to check on Pigeon and make sure she's okay after the hurt fest we just went through, but I stop myself. I'm not ready to open up that channel again. If

I'm being honest, I don't know if I ever will be, and that kills me.

Pigeon is a part of who I am. She was trapped my whole life, and now she's free. I should be celebrating that and strengthening the bond between us like we have been trying to do. But how do I get past the betrayal and the secrets? How do I get past the fact that she didn't tell me? It's like we're two halves working against each other, and I don't know how that can ever work.

Someone pounds on my barricaded door, and I jerk up, startled by the aggression of it. It's either Ryn or Treno, and as much as I'd love to pull a dick move and activate my ghosting skills, we need to talk. Operation Be Mature and Stop Avoiding Shit is now in full effect. I climb out of the tub and quickly dry off as whoever is banging on the other side of the doors shows off their impatience.

"I'm coming! Chill!" I shout out, but I doubt they can hear me over the temper tantrum that's clearly occurring on the other side.

I grab the dress that looks like it'll be the easiest to get into and pull it over my head. Flowing aubergine-colored fabric drops to the floor from my waist, and I tuck my boobs into the deep V of the top. I rush into the main part of the bedroom and find that the impatient knocking has turned into someone trying to shoulder the doors open.

What the hell?

I'm taken aback by someone's effort to get in here, and for a split second, I instinctively reach out to Pigeon. As soon as her consciousness connects with mine, I recoil. I quickly realize what I've done and slam my walls back into place. The doors to my room begin to splinter, and inch by inch my barricade starts to move and make way for whoever is punishing the doors.

I'm not sure if I should help move shit or just wait for

them to muscle their way in. So I just stand there like a statue until I can make out who it is. Another minute of animalistic rage at the door goes on, and then a face as clear as day appears through the broken entrance to my room.

I have no idea who it is.

Panic bubbles up inside of me as a deep voice orders, "Falon Umbra, you are to come with us." He shoves the large table and chairs out of the way, and another colossal guard enters the room. I take an involuntary step back at their advance and try to unfreeze my muscles.

"What's going on?" I ask as each massive male moves to my side.

They wrap their hands around my upper arms, and the next thing I know, I'm being led out of my room and down several hallways and stairs. I'm used to flying in and out of here, and in no time, I'm completely turned around. I have no idea where we are or where we might be going. No one will tell me either, because apparently *that* would be too easy.

We spend what feels like an hour going down stairs, so long in fact that my mind has time to wander and wonder why gryphons even have stairs in their building to begin with. At first I think it's for the elderly or for gryphons who can't fly maybe, but as we round another corner and go down another flight of stone stairs, I no longer think that plausible.

Fucking focus, Falon. Who gives a shit about the stairs, let's give more fucks about why we're being manhandled.

"Where are we going?" I try again, but my guards continue to show their mad skills at the silent treatment.

I try to think through what the catalyst could be for what's happening, but I have no fucking clue, which means my stupid brain just wants to know about the stairs again. We finally exit the step-labyrinth, and the fact that we didn't go as far down as the dungeons gives me a little bit of hope that whatever is going on is going to be okay.

We wind down more halls and past more crystal and iron windows, and a flicker of recognition sparks through me. I think this is the level I was on when I was taken to the massive crystal domed throne room when I first woke up in Kestrel City. I start to recognize more and more, and I suddenly have no doubt that's exactly where I'm being taken. I just still can't figure out why.

The guards stop me in front of the massive iron doors, and I'm forced to wait for them to creak open just like I did that first time. The doors spread with a final irritated boom, and I'm half escorted, half carried in. Unlike last time, most of the thrones are already occupied. Lazza sits in the largest throne in the middle, watching me like a hawk that's going to swoop down from its perch at any moment and make you its dinner.

There's only one female to his left, and she looks bored as fuck. The green-eyed female who marked me is nowhere to be seen and neither is Ryn or some of the old guys that were here last time. Treno is seated on the throne to Lazza's right, and I can't discern what he's thinking or feeling. His face is shuttered. A warning prickle runs up my spine as one of the guards who brought me here steps up to the Syta and whispers something in his ear.

I watch the exchange and try to school my features like Treno is. Something about this scenario is triggering my internal *keep it cool* alarms. The guard steps away and moves somewhere behind me. I watch him go and realize that the big iron doors haven't been closed. It's as if they're expecting more people and don't want to go through the hassle of opening and closing them.

"Why did you have your door barricaded?" Lazza asks

me flatly, and I snap my attention forward, surprised by the question.

Looks like he's not waiting on anyone to get whatever this is started.

"I wanted some quiet time and didn't want to be interrupted," I explain.

It seemed like a perfectly logical thing to do at the time, but I can see that Lazza finds it suspicious for some reason. I look from him to Treno to try and gauge the effect my words might have on him, but he's all steel and hard edges right now. That sends even more worry through me. From the first time I met Treno, after I'd been shot from the sky, netted, and pulled half drowned from the water, he was cheeky and curious. His disguised blue eyes at the time were filled with interest and excitement; now they are just flat and ominous.

"Have you been enjoying your time here, Falon?" Lazza asks me casually.

"I have," I answer, trying to suss out why this feels like a trap.

"I've been informed that you've spent much of your time in the archives, is that correct?" he queries, looking down at his nails like my answer is inconsequential.

Shit. Is this about the mating book I took? Maybe they take that thing more seriously than I thought?

"That's correct," I reply.

"And what have you been looking for in the archives?" he adds.

I answer without hesitation. "I've been looking through the records for information about my parents. I was hoping to find out if they were from here and, if they were, how they ended up in my world." I pause. "I've been trying to make sense of how I got here in hopes that it would help me to get back," I finish.

"Did you discover anything?" he presses, and everything inside of me is screaming do not tell him about your parents.

"No, well, maybe. I came across a name similar to my mother's. I requested additional information, but the archivists haven't found any yet," I offer, hoping the half-truth reads as credible in case anyone in this room can tell.

"Falon, are you a spy for the Hidden?" Lazza asks me simply.

"No," I quickly answer and try to keep my face a mask of confusion instead of showing all the fear that just went slamming through me.

The room grows silent for an uncomfortably long time. Lazza dips his chin, and one of the guards behind me moves. I don't turn to track the guard's movements, too worried if I take my eyes off of Lazza, he'll climb down whatever web he's weaving and string me up. Treno shifts his weight like he's suddenly uncomfortable.

More silence wraps around me, and it feels maddening. When Lazza finally does speak again, I have to keep from jumping, I'm so surprised by it.

"So you're telling me that you don't know him. Is that right, Falon?"

I hear the clang of chains, and I turn to see who Lazza is referring to. Fear was already slamming through me, but when I turn to see Ryn being dragged in by his arms, my fear turns to pure terror. He's been beaten...severely, and it's all I can do not to gasp or start crying.

"Yes, I know him," I admit, taking my eyes off of Ryn and focusing back on Lazza and Treno.

Ryn's life depends on me finding a way to get him out of this, and I'm still not one hundred percent sure exactly what *this* is. The spy question I was asked definitely tips the scales in that direction, but there's still a chance this is somehow about something else. Maybe Treno found out about me and Ryn, and he's not keen on sharing. Who the fuck knows, but I need to figure out how to play this...and fast.

Lazza's eyes light up with interest at my admission, and Treno's narrow.

"This is the Commander you introduced when I first met you. He's also the person who choked me until I blacked out," I add, and Lazza's gaze dims with annoyance.

I try not to look over at Ryn, but it's fucking hard. I can feel Pigeon's agitation even through my barriers. *That*, mixed with my terror, is not a good combination. If I'm not careful, I could slip and give Pigeon control, and then she'd shift and try to fight her way out of here. I can't let her get us all killed unless we have no other choice.

"So you were not aware that he was spying for the Hidden?" Lazza tries again.

This time Treno speaks up, and my heart speeds faster with hope. "Brother, that's my mate you're speaking to," he warns, his voice just above a growl.

Lazza turns to Treno and studies him for a moment. "I have it on good authority that your *mate* is working with the Hidden. I warned you not to seal the bond until we knew more about her," he snaps.

"You keep announcing that you have acquired all of this information *on good authority,* but I've yet to see any proof. You've beaten your Third in command, a male we've known since we were children, and now accuse my mate of being a spy. Stop this tantrum and show me the proof!" Treno bellows, and Lazza's eyes narrow ever so slightly.

"Fine, brother, as you wish." Lazza turns and looks behind me and once again drops his chin.

I sneak a quick glance at Ryn who's holding his side and panting. *Fuck.* He probably has broken ribs and who knows what else. His nose is definitely broken, his eye is black and swollen shut, and the other eye looks like it will be the same way with one more hit. There are gashes and bruises all over him.

I stand there quietly, facing forward and terrified of who or what they'll bring in next. I wonder if Treno can feel my fear or the bile working its way up my throat. Can he feel what I can now that we're bonded? Does he know the truth that my mouth is denying but my body and emotions are confirming?

Pigeon hammers at my walls, something setting her off so completely that she's lost it beyond all recognition. I'm shocked by the violence she uses to smash against me, demanding I give into her. I feel someone step up behind me, and I'm instantly terrified it's Zeph. I feel a sharp blade suddenly being pressed against my throat, and the wielder of the dagger leans down until they're close to my ear.

"Hello, highborn, we meet again."

16

I don't immediately recognize the voice, but the nickname and the smell are a dead fucking give away...Loa.

Rage incinerates every other emotion inside of me, and I seethe. Treno shoots up out of his throne and immediately starts yelling at his brother.

"What is the meaning of this?" he demands, trying to close the distance between us as quickly as possible, but the room is huge.

His throne is positioned at the head of the football-field-and-a-half-long space, and the guards only deposited me halfway between the doors and the thrones. Prisms dance in Treno's hair from the crystal dome above us, and I'd think it was stunning if the psycho traitor bitch, Loa, didn't have a knife to my fucking throat.

I force my face into a mask of fear and confusion. I don't know what she's playing at, but if this is Lazza's source, it's her word against mine.

"Who is this?" Treno demands. "Lazza, I'm warning you right now, order your pet to remove that knife from her throat!"

"Or what?" Lazza calls out. "Loa has more than proved to me the truth of her words. If you refuse to see it, that's not my problem."

He growls, stoppings mid-stride and rounding on Lazza. "You would make an enemy of me today, brother?" he asks on a snarl. "You would accuse my mate of betrayal, threaten her, provide no proof, as is required by our laws, to what end?" Treno demands.

Lazza studies his brother for a second and then huffs. "Lower your knife so my brother can stop thinking with his dick long enough to hear the truth," Lazza orders.

Loa does as she's told and steps to the side of me.

"Looks like you whored yourself out for protection here just like you did in the Eyrie," she growls at me.

Treno and his brother start arguing. I wait until they're both fully consumed with yelling at each other and then drop my voice so only the bitch next to me can hear it.

"If I recall correctly, Loa, I wasn't the one in need of protection. Or did I imagine the Syta stepping in to save your worthless ass?"

She growls at me and turns.

"If you lay one hand on her, I will rip you apart very, very slowly," Treno seethes, and Loa freezes.

"Enough!" Lazza booms, and his voice echoes around the room. "It's time Treno sees the truth."

"Yes, Syta," she chirps.

With that, Loa reaches behind her and threads her fingers through the long black hair at the back of her head. She fumbles with something for a second and then pulls out what looks like a bobby pin with gnarly looking teeth. She throws it on the ground, and it goes skidding toward Treno's feet. It stops about a yard away, and we all just stare at it. I wait to see if it's magically going to morph into video surveillance of me with the Hidden, or maybe it's some kind of voice recording device.

Nothing happens.

Lazza starts to speak, and the hair on the back of my neck and arms stands up. My head snaps in his direction, and fear runs a cold finger up my spine. He's spewing out power words. I recognize the cadence of them immediately, and they wrap themselves around me like old friends to then run off to do whatever it is Lazza is telling them to do. I can practically see the magic pour out of his mouth and slither toward the clip Loa threw on the floor.

A black jewel glints in the light on one end of it as the magic wraps around the object. The jewel starts to smoke, and then all of a sudden like it was made of gun powder, there's a pop and then it turns to ash. I'm still confused by what any of this means, but Loa gives a weird groan, and it pulls me from the whirlwind of questions circling through me.

I look over to find that Loa's face looks wrong. I watch as slowly she morphs from a massive broad-shouldered female, with straight black hair, into a slightly more delicate female with light brown hair and gray eyes.

She looks triumphant as the magic in the room dissipates and the hair pin crumbles into dust on the ground. Treno squints at the revealed visage like he's trying to put it all together.

"Raquel?" he asks hesitantly, his tone bewildered like he can't believe his eyes.

Loa laughs and offers him a wide half-crazed smile that has Pigeon renewing her assault at my defenses.

"How?" Treno demands. "You're dead."

A low growl resonates through the room, and my head snaps in the direction of Ryn. He's still on the ground, but his eyes are fixed on Loa, or Raquel, or whatever her fucking name is.

"Silence, brother, you only have yourself to blame for this," she snaps, and my eyes widen as the connection snaps into place.

I look from Ryn to his sister, and it's impossible now to miss the similarities in their face, hair, and eye color. Loa-Raquel is still too masculine to ever be called pretty, and even with a different face, I still want to rip her fucking guts out.

Treno looks at his brother and then back to Loa-Raquel. "You knew she was alive this whole time?" he asks incredulously.

Lazza rolls his eyes. "I had a chance early on to get someone on the inside. She volunteered, don't look so offended. Things like this only work if you don't tell anyone, so that's exactly what I did. The information she's supplied over the years has saved us and our people many times over. I trust her implicitly, and you should too," he states evenly.

Lazza gestures from Loa-Raquel to Treno. Taking that as her signal to speak, Loa-Raquel opens her mouth and starts selling me out.

"Zeph found her wandering around the Amaranthine Mountains. He brought her back to the old castle that was abandoned outside of Vedan, because she had initiated a call to his gryphon."

"Sound familiar, brother?" Lazza interrupts and asks Treno.

I wish I could leap across this room and punch him. Treno looks to me, and I have to work to keep my face empty. I want to beg him with my mouth and my eyes not to listen. I want to scream for him to wait for me to explain everything so it's not tainted by manipulation and war, but I can't say any of that without risking more than just me.

"Funny enough, he thought she was an Avowed spy. He ordered her cleansed and brought in his little mutt to test her. She passed, but you know Zeph, he doesn't trust anyone except Ryn. He still mated her. From what I hear, she practically forced him to complete the bond. Then she set her sights on my brother. I put a stop to that, and she attacked me out of nowhere for it. Zeph stopped me from killing her, and then she up and went missing. When word trickled down that she had been spotted here, I knew that Zeph was trying to plant another spy," she finishes, shooting me a triumphant look.

I want to roll my eyes at her version of events, but I don't. Instead, I fix Treno with a steady stare. I'm tempted to deny everything, to claim I don't know her. But the truth is, if I do make it out of this...I *will* have to tell Treno the truth. I feel like denying anything now will just set him up to feel even more betrayed, so I say nothing.

"Lazza, I've had enough. Do what you want with Ryn, that's between you and him and your secret spy, but I'm taking my mate and leaving. Raquel's word doesn't hold weight with me like it does with you."

"Don't touch her," Lazza commands, and he stomps toward Treno. "You are not the leader of our people, and you do not give me orders. I am the Syta, and what I say goes. How can you be so shortsighted, Treno? If there's even a small chance that she's mated to Zeph, then we have him by the throat," Lazza growls out.

"And if you're wrong?" Treno counters.

"Then you get your mate back," Lazza replies coolly.

"We both know what you'll put her through to prove one way or another who she's connected to. I can't allow you to do that to her. And how could you want to do that to me? Do you not see my marks on her body? We're bonded!"

Lazza snorts. "It's early. Your gryphons haven't solidified

anything; this is what we've been looking for to end this war. *She* is the key. Sacrifices must be made!"

Treno's mismatched eyes fill with rage and hurt.

"Not like this," he snaps back, taking a threatening step toward his brother.

"Are you challenging me?" Lazza asks on a snarl.

"I'm challenging this decision to hurt my mate all on the word of some chit—"

Out of nowhere, Ryn charges Lazza. I'm frozen, stuck watching it like it's in slow motion, completely torn about what to do. If I jump Loa right now like I want to, Treno will know the truth. It'll gut him. But if I don't help Ryn get out of here somehow, they're probably going to kill him, and I can't let that happen either. I'm fucked no matter what I do.

I take a step toward Loa-Raquel, who has her back to me as she watches Ryn charge the Syta of the Avowed. There's so much space between them that the attack seems futile, but Ryn moves so fucking fast. His body readies itself for attack and starts to morph into his gryphon. I focus on my hand, willing it to partially shift and extend my fingertips into claws.

Lazza's eyes widen and then narrow as he snarls out, *"Tamod hurvas aeyo!"*

Nothing happens, and Ryn slams into Lazza like a freight train, his size and form still changing. Treno sprints in their direction, and then we all freeze as pain filled screams fill the air all around us. The awful, soul-scarring sound wraps itself around me and rips out my heart while also stealing my ability to move or think. I feel a foreign buzzing in my body that doesn't hurt but steals the air from my lungs. I grab at my throat and watch horrified as Ryn rises off of Lazza slowly. His shift stops and his feet lift up off the floor. He's suspended in the air, clawing at his throat and turning purple.

Manic laughter bounces around the crystal walls and ceiling, and Lazza stands up, his eyes crazed and his hand outstretched like he's somehow choking the life out of Ryn.

"You forgot, *old friend*, what I'm capable of," Lazza snarls, spittle and madness spewing from his mouth as he does. "Did you think you'd be immune? That I wouldn't bring you to your knees just like all the others?"

Ryn's clawing at his throat and struggling to stop whatever Lazza is doing to him slowly becomes more sluggish. Tears streak down my face, and black dots form at the corners of my vision. Movement to my right calls to me, and I look over to find Treno bent over, taking pain filled little gasps of air and staring at me, with pure shock and betrayal bleeding out of his gaze.

He knows.

The connection must be forcing him to feel a measure of what I am, and I'm suffocating just like Ryn is. My heart breaks from the pain and confusion I see in Treno's eyes, and I wish I could reach out and steal it all back. I look away and watch Ryn's fight slowly turn into twitches as his body accepts the inevitable death.

Pigeon is slamming into me, keening and lamenting. I can feel her begging to take control, to put a stop to all of this. Lazza is laughing. Loa is staring, her eyes filled with excitement and horror, like she can't decide if watching her brother being murdered is fun or fucking awful. Fire starts in my chest as I internally scream for all of this to stop.

At first I think it's my soul being ripped to shreds, but slowly the fire spreads until it's consumed all of me. It reaches out to the borders of my body like each lick of flame is searing something into the individual cells that comprise...me. It fucking hurts, but it releases the invisible hold on my throat, and I gasp in a lung full of air as the molten heat suddenly condenses inside my chest again like it's ready to explode. Ryn's legs give a final twitch as he hangs in the air, and I turn to Lazza.

I want to shred him. To make sure that no one has to stare into those evil eyes again and face death. I open my defenses to Pigeon. I clear the way for her to take over and do as much damage as she can before they kill us, but it's not Pigeon that surges through me and out into the room. I scream, pain and rage pouring out of me, as a shockwave of purple explodes out of me. It moves through the room, obeying my will and slamming into everyone, blowing them back.

I gape and stare down at my hands as if somehow they belong to someone else. What the fuck was that?

Ryn drops to the ground with a sickening thud, and it snaps me out of my shock and confusion. I stare at him for a beat, but he doesn't move. Dread tears me apart as the words *too late* echo around my head. I rush over to him and place my fingers at his throat and watch his chest. I hold my breath as I try to find the right spot on his neck, the one that will thump rhythmically and give me hope. Tears continue to stream down my face, and they drip onto the filthy shredded tunic he's wearing. Halos of guilt, worry, and pain dapple the fabric as my emotions drip out of my eyes and all over him.

Relief punches through my chest as I finally feel a faint slow rhythm underneath my fingertips. I let out the breath I was holding and watch his chest as if my exhale should become his inhale. My scalp lights up with pain as someone fists a hand in my hair and drags me away from Ryn. I shout out and scramble to try to get to my feet, reaching up to stop the hand from ripping any more chunks out than they already have.

I expect it to be Lazza that I catch in my peripheral, yanking me around, but it's not. It's Loa, and from the brief peeks of her I'm getting, she's well past the edge of enraged.

"Do you see now?" she screams, her voice triumphant and furious.

She swings me around violently, and suddenly I'm facing Treno as he gets to his feet about ten yards away from me. He takes me in, and fear and anger flash in his face. My stomach drops at the rage I see there, and I don't know if there will ever be a way that I can make any of this right.

"Do you have your proof now? That she's one of them...just like I told you she was?" Loa screams at him, and I can't miss the hurt little girl that seems to bleed out of her voice.

I scream for Pigeon, but it feels like she's buried in my head somehow. I can feel her frantically trying to dig herself out and get to me, and I realize I need to buy her time. I focus on my hands and force my talons out.

Loa laughs maniacally next to me, and Treno's face loses color and his eyes go wide with terror. I just spot Lazza out of the corner of my eye nodding, but my attention is ripped away when Treno releases a horrified, "Noooooooo!"

Confused by his reaction, I freeze. Instead of taking a swipe at Loa, I spend a split-second trying to figure out why he wouldn't want me to hurt her.

I realize too late that his anguished scream isn't because of what I'm doing, but because of what Loa is about to do.

17

Warm metal touches my neck. I don't even have time to process that it's a blade before Loa slices across my throat with it.

Pain explodes in my throat, and then I can feel warmth gushing out of me. I try to gasp, but the sound is a sick gurgling that hammers home the reality of what just happened. I press my palms to my slit throat, terrified by how quickly they're covered in blood. I press at the wound and watch as Treno falls to his knees, his large hands clutching his own neck.

The realization that he's experiencing some fucked up echo of what I am flashes through my mind as I press at my wound and wonder how the fuck I'm going to survive this. I blink slowly, and it's as if the world around me has exploded. It's hard to focus, because my mind seems to only want to be aware of the fact that I'm bleeding to death. I feel like I'm moving underwater as I try to comprehend what's happening.

Panes and shards of shattered crystal come raining down from above me, and I fall to my knees, unsure if they are too weak to hold me up anymore or if the strong burst of wind in the room shoved me down. I feel pieces of things fall on me, but all I can really focus on is trying to press the escaping blood from my throat back into my body. I fumble for the skirt of my dress and shakily bring a wad of the fabric up to my throat and press it there.

I'm having trouble breathing, but I can tell some oxygen is getting into my lungs and brain because neither is screaming for air, or maybe my brain is no longer working right because of the blood.

A roar fills the air, but I can't focus on the rage and retribution billowing out and surrounding me. All I can focus on is clumsily pulling more of my dress up and pressing it as hard as I can against my neck. I taste blood in my mouth, and for some reason, it sparks a flash of panic. I try to rein it in, knowing instinctively that keeping my heart rate down is better right now, but it takes root despite my efforts to crush it down.

I don't want to die.

Black talons and skin drop down in my line of sight. They step closer to me, and I can just make out a black paw impossibly far behind the ebony forelegs of what has to be a gargantuan gryphon. I blink lazily, and my vision blurs. Something sniffs at me and nudges me gently, and I can feel strength draining out of my hands. A keening purr kind of a sound reaches out to me, and I want to go to it. More roars and crashes suddenly fill my ears as if someone just unmuted a battle scene in a movie.

I go weightless.

I know I'm dying. I can feel myself rising in the air, like my soul is finally leaving my body. I'm surrounded by warmth and surprisingly...pissed. I've never thought about what it would be like to die, but there's no loved one to greet me. No calm or peace for my soul to float on as I make my way wherever souls go. There's not even a light. There's just pain and guilt and sorrow. All I can think, over and over again, is that I'm sorry any of this happened.

I know my death will pull the others with me, and it feels horrible.

I'm jostled, and my hazy vision blinks out altogether. I grumble internally about how the road to the afterlife shouldn't have potholes. This shit should be gentle and easy; why does it hurt? Something wraps around me, and then the sensation of flying fills the last of my working senses. Peace finally trickles through me, but so does panic because this must be it.

I don't want to die!

Everything around me grows quiet, and in spite of the cool wind I feel caressing my body, I'm warm all over. A flash of Ryn, then Treno, and finally Zeph streaks by the last of my consciousness before I can feel it finally start to shut down. I whimper, and death squeezes me tighter.

"Don't worry, little sparrow, I have you," it growls deeply into my ear, and then everything...goes...black.

The End of Book Two...

ALSO BY IVY ASHER

The Sentinel World

THE LOST SENTINEL

The Lost and the Chosen

Awakened and Betrayed

The Marked and the Broken

Found and Forged

SHADOWED WINGS

The Hidden

The Avowed

The Reclamation

MORE IN THE SENTINEL WORLD COMING SOON.

Paranormal Romance

HELLGATE GUARDIAN SERIES

Grave Mistakes

Grave Consequences

Grave Decisions

Grave Signs

THE OSSEOUS CHRONICLES

The Bone Witch

Book 2 coming soon

Shifter Romantic Comedy Standalone

Conveniently Convicted

Dystopian Romantic Comedy Standalone

April's Fools

ABOUT THE AUTHOR

Ivy Asher is addicted to chai, swearing, and laughing a lot—but not in a creepy, laughing alone kind of way. She loves the snow, books, and her family of two humans, and three fur-babies. She has worlds and characters just floating around in her head, and she's lucky enough to be surrounded by amazing people who support that kind of crazy.

Join Ivy Asher's Reader Group and follow her on Instagram and BookBub for updates on your favorite series and upcoming releases!!!

facebook.com/IvyAsherBooks
instagram.com/ivy.asher
bookbub.com/profile/ivy-asher
amazon.com/author/ivyasher

Printed in Great Britain
by Amazon